T0149746

THE
IMMEDIATE
EXALTED TASK

JOHN HERSHEY

authorHOUSE®

AuthorHouse™
1663 Liberty Drive
Bloomington, IN 47403
www.authorhouse.com
Phone: 1 (800) 839-8640

Holy Bible, New International Version®*, NIV*® *Copyright* ©*1973, 1978, 1984, 2011 by*
http://www.biblica.com/ Biblica, Inc.® *Used by permission. All rights reserved worldwide.*

Published by AuthorHouse 06/28/2018

ISBN: 978-1-5462-4708-1 (sc)
ISBN: 978-1-5462-4707-4 (e)

CONTENTS

ACKNOWLEDGEMENTS

Thomas Merton, title suggestion

Kate H and Tom C, proofing help

ONE

MISE-EN-SCÈNE

THE WEIGHT OF FORTY-PLUS MINNESOTA WINTERS

In February the weight of forty-plus Minnesota winters defeats Micah Hardy. His soul wilts.

He no longer counts the season's accumulation of sub-zero nights. The handful of sub-zero days adds insult. After frost gnaws the exposed tip of his right ear Hardy goes on strike. When he doesn't have to go outside he refuses to. *Too damn cold.* It's what he replies when asked to stand in the evening air to view the rare Super Blue Blood Moon.

The debilitating fatigue and stiffness he experiences in the wake of too many driveway snow clearing forays also contributes to his collapse. He assumed the shoveling chore after his housemate wrenched a previously injured lower back.

Hardy still wears the bruises he acquired from an ungraceful tumble on sidewalk ice. His shoulder aches constantly with the cold. The long-vacated chilly Other Side of the Bed makes his heart ache.

The truth is basic. The accumulated load of cold, frostbite, shovel fatigue, black and blue marks, aching joints, loneliness and a dispirited attitude does him in.

Then during a notably frigid hike to work Hardy fixates on an image a good friend attaches to a recent email. His smiling buddy triumphantly displays a thirty-inch redfish he's pulled out of a Florida

Gulf Coast backwater with a fly rod. Hardy's imagination briefly transports him to that subtropical location as he crunches along a snowy path.

Somewhere right now there's a guy standing on the bow of a flats boat. He's wearing shorts. He's casting a big fly toward a cruising tarpon.

In that Arctic Instant Micah Hardy vows to change his life.

He breaks out laughing and a sidewalk passerby gapes. He considers his vow. One he's made a thousand times. He knows he doesn't possess the energy or the gumption to make any lifestyle revision. Instead he yanks open his office building door and resumes his rightful place on a familiar treadmill.

He does not know the winds of change stir. Much like a hurricane developing in the Atlantic off the African coast.

TWO

A GOOD STORY

I HOPE YOU KEEP TURNING PAGES

"That's a good story."

It's what I say when I appreciate the one you tell me.

It's what I hope this is. A good story.

I'll start by thanking you for reading. Not many do. I hope you keep turning the pages. I hope to engage you without insulting your intelligence. I hope you want to find out what happens next, what happens at the end.

As far as discovering what happens at the end? I hope I do too.

Don't read too much into what you find here. There are no deep messages. I address no substantive themes, literary or otherwise. I wrestle with no significant social issues. I have no axe to grind. There are no titillating self-revelations. This is the stuff of Everyday Life. I merely beef it up.

I've got a decent imagination.

The events herein described are not real. The sets are fabricated. I've long wanted to write about a place I invented in my mind. I call it *The House on the Hill*. It's featured in the first novel I ever wrote. One I produced in my mid-twenties. No surprise I lost it given how stoned I used to get. You're lucky you're not reading *The Wedding at Cana* here.

The characters are likewise the stuff of invention. Many are female. I like girls more than boys. They're more interesting. More apt to tell you what they're thinking, how they're feeling.

What interests me about these players is by naming them they've taken residence in my mind. They walk with me during the day. Sometimes they keep me awake at night. Sometimes they appear in my dreams.

I no longer need to speak for them. They've begun talking to me and I have learned to listen. They say and do things I don't know I'm going to write until I hear them say it or watch them do it. I suspect they're going to take me places I haven't yet discovered.

If you're willing to turn the page let's visit Micah Hardy. He likes a good story. He's not very good at telling his own. I'm out to change that.

THREE

SPIRITUAL BOX CANYON

WHAT YOU NEED TO KNOW

Let me introduce Micah Hardy.

He is a good man.

He knows he lives a life of White Male Privilege. He doesn't know how guilty he should feel about it.

He pays his bills on time and his life insurance is paid in full.

He doesn't carry a credit card balance. Ever.

He gives an honest work place effort.

He is circumspect, keeps opinions to himself. Feelings too. Definitely feelings.

He'll remember your name. Open the door for you.

He delivers Meals on Wheels; distributes goodie bags to street corner homeless.

He recycles. He owns and uses a compost bin.

He picks up stray street trash, collects river bank rubbish.

He shops local, belongs to a co-op and mostly eats organic but can't take much credit for it. Noir does the marketing and cooking. You'll meet her if you keep reading. She's an intelligent and feisty young woman. She loves old movies.

Hardy obeys speed limits, always buckles up.

He supports worthy charities, notably ones conducting cancer research.

He loves basketball, the out-of-doors. And dogs.

He's an amateur ornithologist.

He fishes with flies for trout.

You'd describe him like you would a homely girl you want your friend to date: All his friends like him.

He's good in many ways. Except to himself. Phrased gently, he is not living a Genuine Life.

Bluntly put? He lives a lie.

He loathes city living.

He despises his job.

Hardy's a community and government relations guy for the College of St. Rose, a Catholic school that lost its religion. He not only cleans up the excrement the institution deposits in its tracks, he produces it. He owns a talent for creating his own version of Institutional Baloney, which he freely dispenses. Check out his website. His job is to be nice about helping St. Rose get what it wants.

Sometimes whether citizens want it or not.

Sometimes whether he's nice or not. Sometimes he plays hardball.

It's after midnight and the house is silent. Hardy's reading a favored fly-fishing writer who recounts an entry into community politics and subsequently discovers he's wandered into a Spiritual Box Canyon. The author entered the Community Arena with the best of intentions but, to achieve his goal, he wound up pulling a political trigger like a Ruthless Assassin.

The situation rings as true and clear as brass prayer bells to Hardy. He gasps, deeply affected by the writer's clarity of expression. He sets the book aside and contemplates his Personal Box Canyon. His dislike for his job, his empty spiritual life.

He ponders the reality of his existence from the vantage of seven decades. An inertia-plagued life. He keeps a job because it pays the bills, contributes to his retirement and provides medical coverage. He's played it safe and walked the easy path, one others expected him to follow. He's lived an orderly life. An electron faithfully orbiting its nucleus.

What did it get him? Not much.

An ancient four-wheel Suburban.

A snowblower that starts first-time every-time.

Eight fly rods and too many flies.

Clothes to last until he travels Up Yonder.

A home he shares with a pair of renegade friends in a forty-five-degree latitude American city where summer swelters under steamy dew points and winter freezes your Gorgonzolas off.

A wife who left him. She says he doesn't Believe Right. She can't live with a man who's not authentically Christian.

Deep down? Hardy suspects he never believed at all.

He's happy to have a happily married daughter. She and hers live nearby. They talk to him.

A daughter somewhere else doesn't. This grates, but like most guys he's a stubborn and prideful blockhead. He refuses to talk about it. He'd have to tell you how he feels.

The sobering reality arrows into Hardy's heart as late winter sleet pings against the window. Who owns the hands resting lightly in his lap? Whose age-spotted mitts are corrugated with veiny relief maps?

Hardy grips a cool bottle of Grain Belt, lifts it, tilts and dispatches the remaining lager. A line from a vintage Talking Heads album drifts into his mind.

"How did I get here?"

The innocent question brings focus, irks him.

I will begin to answer that question now and I have an idea I might get help along the way. You might encounter a series of storytellers as we proceed but let's not put the cart before the horse. In *The Wizard of Oz*, Glinda, the Good Witch of the North, tells Dorothy, "It's always best to start at the beginning."

This is what Kirkallen would tell you too. He's the injured housemate. He'll tell you a Navajo typically solves a problem by beginning at the Alpha Point. Keep reading and you'll find out more about Kirkallen and his Navajo Phase.

You'll also meet Hardy's wife, his daughters, Noir and a host of others. For the moment however? Let's walk for a while in Hardy's shoes.

We'll get to the lake eventually.

Check it out. Hardy's drifting in his recliner. He's going to dream he left his job to follow a shapely dark haired woman he can see from behind, dimly in the distance. She's wearing a billowing white dress and a wide brimmed straw hat.

GIVE HIM THE NEEDLE

"How's the shoulder?" Doc Stone asks.

I close my book and stand to greet my orthopedist. Doc is brusque and direct. A typical male doctor. He is younger than I but that's not saying much. It's obvious he colors the brown hair he's clearly pleased to comb. He sports the Country Club Look comfortably and without pretense. His eyebrows need trimming. Like mine.

My mind wanders. *Is there a Special Someone who helps Doc with personal grooming? I don't see any family photos in his office. He doesn't talk about a wife. Let alone kids.*

Doc's a fisherman. He can afford the fly-fishing destination trips I take on YouTube. It's by Talking Fishing we've achieved an easy, less formal relationship, including his rueful admission to a fallen chest and the inability to keep to regular exercise. And including my rueful response to his question, *You still get it up?*

I sit and dispense with preliminaries. "Doc, I've been avoiding the cortisone but I woke up the other night and my shoulder hurt like a mother …"

"… Hell," the physician amends my sentence direction.

His smartphone sounds a Beatles tune from their pre-psychedelic days. He removes it from a belt holder. "I'm on call." He shrugs an apology and steps into the hall. "Yes?" The door whispers shut.

I am abandoned in a sterile antiseptically scented room and to the muffled White Noise Hum of a physician's office.

This day I'd arrived agreeably early, agreeably completing a medical update form offered by an agreeably middle aged and comely office manager after I agreeably peered down at her exposed cleavage and lavender bra. And yes she caught me *in flagrante.*

"Adele," I apologized, "I'm a guy. What can I say?"

"Not to worry, Mr. Hardy," she responded. "It's not like I don't know you. Besides you're really tall and this morning my husband wasn't home and my kids …" she held her tongue and averted her eyes as if pondering how much to divulge about a wayward husband and needy children. She changed tack. "I dressed in a hurry, left home in a tizzy. I typically don't wear V-necks to work."

She rested her forearms on the desk and sheepishly aimed her thumbs toward her bosom and tugged at her shirt to achieve an additional modicum of modesty. She offered a coy smile. "I'm flattered a gentleman like you would notice. Men don't stare like they used to."

I laughed. "Gentleman? Hardly. You saw where my eyes went. One of my housemates is seriously into old movies. She has a grand memory for quotes. She threw this one at me the other day. Something Lana Turner said. 'A gentleman is simply a patient wolf.'"

We left it there, each slightly embarrassed and flushing pink.

I never go the doctor's office without a book. There's always a wait and I like reading. I don't mind having time to do it. While Doc talks on his cell I bury my nose in a mystery featuring a protagonist who smokes reefer. I like him. I'm also jealous. I haven't tasted *ganja* in years.

The door opens. "Any good?" Stone points to the paperback.

I angle the cover toward him. "It's entertaining. A Mafia-type thriller on steroids. There are shoot-outs and guys bleed and die and dames take off their clothes."

"You like mysteries?"

"Not usually. I've worked through that phase. What I like is a writer who talks to me and keeps me turning pages."

"You're lucky you know something you like." It's a regretful confession.

Doc shifts gears. "Ever read a guy named West? He's a patient. Lives on Summit Avenue. He does a decent mystery. Him and the guy who made a name for himself by writing early mornings at The Broiler. What's his name?"

"Krueger. William Kent Krueger. The Broiler closed. They couldn't compete without selling a decent meal for less than one of Krueger's mysteries."

I don't mention to Doc he shouldn't be sharing a patient's name.

"Check out West," he says. He scribbles the name and a title on a prescription slip and slides it into my book and redirects. "Talk to me about your shoulder."

"It wakes me up and I've been trying to ignore the pain but I woke up the other night and said to myself *I want the needle.*"

"We should get you an MRI."

"We did. Last winter."

I omit confiding: *No one ever called with the results.*

"Oh … right." Doc thinks for a moment and crow's-feet crowd the corners of his eyes. "Shoulder like yours?" he offers. "Maybe you have a slight tear. You definitely have a lot of bone spurs and I don't like you getting all these cortisone injections. I could 'scope it but it might not be worth the cost and aggravation."

I resist the temptation to remind him about the last time we talked about getting too many injections and he said *We ought to try something different. Like surgery.*

"I didn't come here asking for trouble. Trout season's open. I don't want to mess up my casting with an operation. Let's keep it simple. Give me the shot."

"Well," Docs says thoughtfully, "you're sixty-two-ish?"

I nod.

"Statistically you've got about eighteen years left. So until the pain gets to you or you get too old to wade and stop casting it seems like a shot at three-month intervals is the way to go. You okay with our plan?"

"Sign me up." The thought of Not Casting gives me the willies.

"Done. Off with your shirt." Doc rises. He pats my knee, a paternal gesture. "I'll ask Adele to schedule you in about three months? See you then? And try the West. He'll keep you turning pages."

Stone opens the door and beckons to his male nurse as he leaves. "Give him the needle," he says quietly.

It sounds like a directive to put a dog to sleep.

HE KNOWS HE DOESN'T HAVE MANY SEASONS LEFT

I'll confide an additional truth about Micah Hardy. Notice how he didn't say anything to Doc about how they'd been through the same Song and Dance Diagnosis, the identical surgery suggestion and a Xerox prescription for an ongoing treatment plan?

Hardy has no talent for personal confrontation. Especially if it includes sharing his feelings. But give him a college to fight for? He'll stand toe to toe with you.

He keeps his Business Self separate from his Personal Self.

Often to the detriment of the latter.

He also told Stone he didn't want surgery because it would mess with his trout fishing. That part is true. He knows he doesn't have many seasons left until he'll be too frail to wade. He fears he might need to resort to playing golf.

It's a doubly repugnant notion. He thinks golf courses are Water Thieves, wasters of a precious and unrenewable resource. He also can't abide the notion of paying a greens fee to wait in line at a tee in order to enjoy the outdoors.

Hardy wants the needle, not the knife.

What he omitted entirely from the conversation? He is deathly afraid of doctors and hospitals.

Hardy can barely stomach a medical appointment. He's afraid a physician will discover Something Else Wrong. Then there was the last man he saw go into a hospital. He came out the back door zipped inside a black bag.

His father. Hardy had the honor of giving the word to pull the Life Support Plug.

Micah Hardy thinks another name for *hospital* is *morgue*.

Notice too, Hardy took absolutely no offense to Doc's comment about Eighteen Years Left. The clinical reference to an American Male's average life span. A woman might've taken it as an outrageous affront.

We'll have to wait to see how Hardy feels about that. Or if it even registered.

Keep reading and we'll find out. We can begin by checking in with him in the next chapter.

A KIND OF INVISIBLE MAN

"We have to stop meeting like this," I say to the entering assistant. "It's like you're my junkie." I grin at the laconic man.

He understands my lame attempt at humor is a way of masking Needle Anxiety. He owns the grace to curb his tongue.

I'm also distracting myself from thinking about taking my shirt off in front of him. These days I despise it. I'm old. Soft in more places than I want to be soft.

You know that thought's headed to the gutter. Let's skip ahead.

Like Doc, my chest has fallen. My sagging gelatinous whiteness is exaggerated in the exam room's unkind light. I look ridiculous. The less you see of me the better.

The tech is shorter than I. Most people are since I'm six-seven. He wears a navy scrub top over a light blue bottom. His running shoes gleam blindingly white. I resist the urge to tramp on them.

He exudes a gay vibe. Not that it matters. I'm only telling you I have an Extra Radar Screen. I don't know why.

He slips on latex gloves making me feel like a leper. I silently yearn for the Old Days when Doc Shea unceremoniously shoved his hand into my mouth and went about his dental excavating with a foot-pump drill.

The tech eases behind me, discretely filling the syringe. "Did the injection provide any relief last time, Mr. Hardy?"

"Not as long as I wanted."

He apologizes for requiring a step stool and stands on it. "This will sting."

I distract myself by reading the poster on the wall and burst out laughing as I welcome the uncomfortable tingle of the cortisone infusion.

"You okay?"

"I'm good. No worries. I've been in this office a bunch of times but I never checked out the poster."

"The Health Pyramid?"

"I can't do anything about the two basic cornerstones."

"Socioeconomic Status and Genetics," the assistant fills in.

"Nutrition, Regular Exercise, the stuff up at the pyramid top, they don't contribute significantly to the equation, huh?"

"You said it, not me."

"Why get this shot? Why not proceed directly to the single malt?"

He extracts the needle and doesn't respond. "You're good to go."

"Thanks, man. I'll see you again."

"Probably. But stay away from taking the single malt in excess."

We exit the office one behind the other. I leave my completed questionnaire on the chair. The one I agreeably completed for the agreeable Adele. I silently vow not to complete the next one.

Adele hands me an appointment card for a visit three months hence. She promises to send an email too. She doesn't say she suspects I'll lose the card.

"I'll put the date on my calendar," she flirts. "I want to remember to wear a low-cut blouse."

Her smile illuminates the room. It is one of the two best moments of my day.

Her Smile and The Glimpse of Adele's Lavender Bra.

What does that say about the Medical Profession?

The highlight of my visit to an orthopedist is a gratuitous glance down a receptionist's blouse and subsequently enjoying her flirtatious smile?

Here's the long and short of it. My entire specialist visit took less than five minutes. Well, ten with the interruption. It will cost about two hundred bucks, another three bills for the shot. I should've spent the money on a new Sage fly rod I won't let myself buy. Jameson's finest could easily dull the pain. In the long run the rod would make me feel a heck of a lot better.

I'm leaving the doctor's office thinking I've wasted my time—and with the feeling I've been looked through, not seen. A kind of Invisible Man.

I'll ponder the notion as I head to work.

"Jesus, I need to go fishing."

I'm not sure who said that but there you have it.

I don't disagree.

ADELE FROWNS

The glance down Adele's blouse might just be the best moment of Micah Hardy's day. It's about to get a whole lot worse. Or depending on the lens you employ maybe a whole lot better. Let's see.

Adele frowns when she reads Hardy's Out of Office response to her appointment reminder. She steps away from her desk and catches the orthopedist in the hallway. "Dr. Stone?"

Stone pirouettes at the sound of her voice. "Yes."

"Does Micah Hardy still work at St. Rose?"

"I think so. He didn't say anything to the contrary. I didn't ask. We talked about books."

"That's odd," Adele rejoins.

"What's odd?"

"I sent an email appointment reminder to him and it bounced back with a message about Mr. Hardy not working at St. Rose anymore."

"That is odd," Stone remarks offhandedly. His mind is focused on his next patient.

"So is he." Adele adds, "The only guy I know who's ever admitted to peeking down my blouse. But he is kind of cute. For an Old Guy."

That's Micah Hardy for you. Like him or not you remember he passed your way. Six-seven can do that to you.

SITTING IN LIMBO

Hardy is idling in his aged Chevy Suburban casually minding his own business at an Urban Intersection. He taps his foot to a reggae beat, *The Harder They Come* soundtrack, and considers the rear bumper appliqué in front of him.

Does everyone's job suck or just mine?

Hardy ponders his own Specific Professional Frustrations. A public relations job for a college whose profit ethic he disdains.

Reduced to its essentials Hardy walks behind his employer with a pooper scooper and a can of air freshener. No sanitary gloves though. He gets dirty. Scurrilous invective is often heaped on him at public meetings.

Why? He represents the college's greed.

He is evil personified.

The CD morphs into Jimmy Cliff's *Sitting in Limbo* as Hardy ponders the bull he's peddled at the bidding of the College of St. Rose. He smiles at the recollection of the sole off-color joke his father ever shared. One about a newly arrived missionary addressing an African tribe, its members responding with an enthusiastic *hazangah* to each pledge he made to improve their quality of living.

After he finished speaking and walked away from the group the missionary glowed with pleasure at his warm welcome. Then his interpreter advised him to avoid stepping in the *hazangah* deposited on the dusty road by a wandering quadruped.

The Chevy's wipers labor against the April wintry mix rapidly acquiring a wintrier attitude.

Stuck at the light, stuck between Where He Is and What He Doesn't Know He Wants, Hardy allows the song to describe his life.

"Sitting here in limbo waiting for the tide to turn."

This is the moment Doc's Eighteen Years Left comment kicks in. It does not upset or offend.

Hardy interprets it as a Wake-Up Call.

His own voice startles him.

"Invisible at sixty-two! Stuck in a dead-end job. If you're not where you want to be it's your own damn fault. You've got plus-or-minus eighteen years to live. Why don't you grow a pair?"

The song continues. "Sitting here in limbo waiting for the tide to flow. Sitting here in limbo knowing that I have to go."

"I need to start using what time and health I have left," he utters. "Time to turn in my resignation."

It's not an idea. It's a given.

THIS IS ABOUT TO GET UGLY

An impatient horn blares and transports Micah Hardy to the present. He's daydreaming at a green light. He depresses the accelerator and continues, aware the motorist behind him assumes a Distracted by Texting Delay. No way to explain the Deep Thoughts he was considering.

He steers into campus, locates a rare open parking space and exits the vehicle. He stands a moment in the precipitation. There's an honest and raw feel to it—as opposed to the artificial light and air of Doc Stone's office. Leaving the car unlocked he trudges toward his LaSalle Hall work place.

A uniformed campus officer interrupts his progress immediately inside the front door. "Mr. Hardy?" the pert and sturdy woman queries.

"Yes?"

"Come with me, please?"

Hardy proves he can read a name badge. "What gives, Officer Erickson?"

The uniformed woman studies the toes of her glossy boots. "I'm following orders. I'm not privy to the details, sir."

Hardy snorts derisively, "I've been following orders for as long as I can remember."

Cognizant she has no clue regarding the Recent Revelatory Antecedents prompting his reaction and remark he nonetheless continues. "See where it's gotten me? Following directions? Taking the Safe Path? Take a lesson, officer. Find your muse and follow."

"Yes, sir," the woman responds. She's got a job to do. "Why don't you come with me? Please?"

She gestures for him to walk and clanks along beside him, her work belt outfitted with a cornucopia of law enforcement tools. The snow is changing to rain and they raise their collars against it. While Erickson avoids direct conversation she does apologize for failing to provide an umbrella. They stride briskly across the granitically attractive and stolid campus toward Erasmus Hall, home to the College Big Wigs. Central Administration.

"No way you could comfortably carry an umbrella on your belt," Hardy quips as he enters the door she holds for him. They pause to shake the moisture off their coats and troop up a three flights of marble stairs.

On the fourth floor they enter the provost's suite where Erickson knocks on a rear door to Gayle Harte's office. It swings open after the officer swipes a card through an electronic lock.

"Ah, Mr. Hardy. Welcome."

A heavy set woman with straw-like hair, black eyeliner and eyes gleaming with the intensity of a peregrine in stoop is ensconced behind a massive desk, its top furnished solely with an outsized laptop.

Provost Gayle Harte.

Harte takes a deep breath and rises to greet him, arranging a volume of gaudy loose fitting clothing about her and gesturing toward a chair on which rests a navy folder embossed with the St. Rose seal. She does not extend her hand but deferentially asks the officer to stand circumspectly against the wall.

"To witness the conversation," she states formally while nodding at angle to an additional attestée. Dean Elaine Gillespie perches tensely nearby in a straight-back.

Hardy settles uneasily and gives an involuntary shudder. *I'd hate to see this chick with her clothes off.*

He says, "Somehow I don't think this is going to be a genuine conversation but I'm all ears."

This is about to get ugly.

I'm merely the writer here. The raconteur. It's my job to know when to step off the path and let the characters take over. Better to listen to them talk than for me to transcribe. We know Hardy's a reticent fellow. We also know he's after experiencing a life altering Damascus Road Moment. Let's check out his perspective.

AN UPSIDE-DOWN BIRD

I learned to work around Gayle Harte's unfortunate God-given mien unfortunately underscored by her disagreeably sharp tongue and penchant for placing her large shoe into an equally large mouth. When I couldn't avoid a Face-to-Face with the provost I imagined speaking with Grace Kelly in her beautiful Hitchcock days.

So comely and pure I wouldn't dare undress her.

Whereas with say a young Lauren Bacall in *Key Largo*? I'd undress her in a heartbeat.

I found it easier to converse with an imagined Grace Kelly than a real Gayle Harte.

To this day I'm not sure what I did to cause offense upon Provost Harte's administrative arrival at St. Rose. Other than accepting a paycheck and possessing the penis and scrotum she couldn't own. It didn't take long to understand she didn't much like men. At least ones she couldn't control. The latter group compelled her to find the means to slice their figurative nuts off. Failing that she provided them with sufficient restrictive workplace caveats to limit their effectiveness.

We got off on the wrong foot when I strenuously resisted her stipulating my attendance at a public relations seminar to, as she put it, *Acquire the requisite skills to deliver Our Corporate Message.*

Since when did St. Rose *need* a Corporate Message? I thought I worked for a college.

I needed to learn how to get what St. Rose wanted without appearing to want it. And okay I admit it. I enjoyed busting her chops and resisted manipulation.

Gradually I learned to guard my tongue. I kept my peace at meetings necessitating our mutual attendance and adopted an avoidance game plan, convening as obliged and holding the image of Young Grace in my mind. I responded to her when directly addressed but generally chose to fly beneath her radar screen.

This is the first time I've been called Front and Center.

I have a good idea why.

She swivels at her desk and stares out the window tenting her fingers under her nose as she regards a small slate-and-white bird creeping down a quadrangle oak.

"A white-breasted nuthatch," I offer by identifying the black capped bird wearing blue-gray plumage over its descriptive chest. "Most call it an upside-down bird for its ability to creep headlong down a tree. Other woodpecker-types back down trees. A nuthatch doesn't use its tail as a balance point."

Harte shifts in her chair. Her mouth falls open in disbelief.

"Upside-down," I offer lamely. I ponder the bumper sticker revelation I'd experienced earlier, "Kinda like my life?"

I shrug.

"Mr. Hardy," the woman begins, "I didn't invite you here today for an ornithology lesson nor do I have the slightest interest in assessing the state of your life. Why don't we cut to the chase?"

She motions toward the folder in my lap.

"Given the circumstances delineated in the enclosed documents I'm prepared to accept your resignation."

My mouth says it before my mind thinks it. "I don't know whether to curse you or kiss you."

As an afterthought I add, "What circumstances?"

YOU CAN'T HAVE ENOUGH FRIENDS

It's accurate to say my interview with Gayle Harte doesn't improve. Especially after her preposterous racist accusation about Malcolm and the Candy Bar.

I really throw her off her game when I refer to an old Peter, Paul & Mary song about a San Francisco hippie who tried to give a candy bar to a kid and got accused of being a pervert.

"What on earth are you talking about?" she quizzes. She's momentarily distracted but resumes an obviously rehearsed presentation. "Given this unfortunate interpersonal circumstance I view the present as a Perfect Time for a Change. You know we have a new president coming on board for the next fiscal year. I'd like to give him the chance to begin with a clean slate as far as Community and Government Relations is concerned."

We continue our downhill slide after I inform her she can take my job and shelve it next to her Positive Corporate Message. The one omitting any reference to St. Rose's Catholic Mission.

Harte raises her left eyebrow and motions to our wincing witnesses. "Will you both note the particularly caustic reference, please?"

Refocusing on me she grins. "We've finally arrived on the same page in the text. We actually agree on one item. Removing your name from the St. Rose employee roster."

"I doubt we've ever been on the same page. We read different books," I reply.

She is flustered. She points to the door. "Well … I … ahh … we … we will reconvene soon. I look forward to it. With our cards on the table I'm certain we can arrive at an Amicable Separation Agreement."

Amicable Separation Agreement? I heard the same thing from my wife. This is getting contagious.

As I'm leaving Harte mentions she'll be certain to include Dean Gillespie in our next encounter, "To bear witness to our continued conversation."

"Makes perfect sense," I remark. "It's crucial to cover the Corporate Butt. I've learned that much about Corporate Messaging."

Harte ignores the jibe and once more motions to the door.

She beckons to a bewildered Officer Erickson and asks her to escort me to my office. "Please provide Mr. Hardy with a brief but adequate time to collect his effects. His computer accounts and electronic access are frozen. No need to tarry."

I'm directed to remove my belongings and steer clear of campus and I request permission to keep my workout privileges at the gym and she says *Not on your life.*

"We'll speak again soon, Mr. Hardy."

"Since I'm no longer welcome on campus I guess we'll have to speak off campus then? How about lunch at the new French place on Grand? On you, I presume?"

My escort opens the door and motions for me to exit. Coincidentally we pass Malcolm as we depart. He's pushing a vacuum over the corridor carpet. I greet him with a smile, call him *Mr. Morrison.* He averts his eyes and I experience an intolerable sadness.

I've lost a friend.

I know about Malcolm's life, about his Indiana childhood. We spoke often and at length in late afternoons when he entered my office to empty the trash and tidy up.

You can't have enough friends in this world.

I rapidly cram sundry office items into a Franklin Co-op cloth shopping bag. Thirty years doesn't amount to much.

Officer Erickson and I leave my place of employ for the final time. As we walk down the hallway she voices an unkind comment about my ex-supervisor which closes with, "For all you've done for this place? The least she can do is let you use the gym."

We emerge into refreshing air under the assault of heavy wet flakes. I stand to one side to allow entry to a female student who shields her hair with an upraised coat. She sports black tights and a scooped close-fitting top.

I greet her, "Good afternoon."

She fails to respond. Her ears are stuffed with headphone buds.

Young women wearing tights. Their accentuated shapes leading the curious male eye.

The Creator's gift to sixty-ish men. No doubt.

Though girls frequently doffed their tops in my college years there's mystery in speculating about something you can't quite see—and at my age can't do anything other than appreciate the art form.

I know I shouldn't think these thoughts. But I'm a guy.

There you have it.

NEVER TALKED THAT WAY

Wow.

The first thing you need to understand is I'd never talked that way to Gayle Harte. Never talked like that to anyone really—except perhaps in jest to close friends.

That thing about the nuthatch? Bizarre, huh?

Thank goodness I didn't voice my thought about not wanting to see her naked. Jesus.

I'm not sure where my filter went but it up and split. Comments kept coming out of my mouth. Kind of like when I idled at the stop light earlier today. The stuff about being *Invisible at sixty-two* and turning in my resignation?

That came out of the blue too.

I surprised myself more than I surprised Gayle Harte and Dean Gillespie. Did my long-missing twin brother speak for me? Whoever spoke certainly wasn't The Me I Know. I'm the kind of guy who holds his tongue. I veil my astonishment, keep a straight face, weigh the facts and respond circumspectly.

The best I can tell you is visiting my doctor's office, reading a bumper sticker and listening to a *Harder They Come* soundtrack served as, can I use the Narrator's biblical reference here?, a *Damascus Road Moment*.

The one where Saul the Jew becomes Paul the Apostle. With a complete character change the guy goes on to become probably the most influential figure in early Christianity besides Jesus himself.

Think for a moment about Paul's conversion. Even though there are three Gospel versions the basics are the same. He walks out of one town, hears a heavenly voice and strolls into the next village a changed man.

If I told that same tale? You'd say I was delirious, right? Maybe doing drugs? Yet that's what I think I'm telling you. I'm becoming a different person. Like Paul.

Maybe even the Person I Can Truly Be.

You know the Narrator, the writer who's been talking to you, telling you what I'm thinking and doing and feeling? I'm moving him into the back seat.

He'll do spot duty mostly because he needs to keep this narrative moving. But from this moment forward I'll try to talk to you *sans* interpreter. I'll see if I can get others to talk too. I have some interesting friends. The only thing I have to watch out for—and I think the Narrator knows this—is to keep Kirkallen from talking. He talks too much.

As we continue, understand this. Telling you what I think and feel? This is new territory.

Let's begin with Malcolm. It's an easy and obvious place for me to start. I'm not a betting man but if you've come along with me I'm wagering you're interested in knowing about Malcolm and the Candy Bar.

HERSHEY'S EXTRA DARK

I befriended a janitor, a gentleman who cleaned my office. Malcolm stood tall and trim and serious and black. During work breaks he watched the cable in the outer office, a room where my colleagues and I monitored newscasts to ensure items involving St. Rose befitted our Corporate Message.

Malcolm didn't give a hoot about Message. He tuned to religious channels. He listened to the preachers. Sometimes I did too.

He liked to talk. I'm pretty good at listening. It's easier to listen than it is to talk.

Malcolm owns Indiana roots—brothers and sisters, aunts and uncles, cousins, grandparents, a handful of whom struggle to walk the Straight and Narrow. His mother disappeared during his grammar school years, reappearing in his maturity. She lives in Joplin, Missouri, sings alto in a church choir and cashiers for a grocery chain. She visits on occasion.

Malcolm puts up with it. He figures his kids should meet their grandmother and draw their own conclusions. He tries to keep a charitable attitude about her as the Good Book says he ought to. He humbly acknowledges the occasional lapse.

Though Malcolm knew his Bible backward and forward, his father publicly proclaimed the Gospel. A Coca Cola delivery man by day Malcolm's dad preached Wednesday nights and weekends. Malcolm got his goodness from his daddy. His faith too.

"He was my mother and father," Malcolm confided. "He taught me Scripture, cooked my meals, washed my clothes, read me books and made sure I went to school and church. Most of all he kept me away from trouble. I loved that man."

Whenever Malcolm mentioned his father he eventually got around to the end.

His tone capitalized the action, the strength of his beliefs and the destination. "He's Crossed Over. I miss him but I know I'll see him on the Other Side."

What a comforting thought.

I told Malcolm I wished I had faith as strong as his.

The only *Other Side* I can imagine has a healthy trout stream running through it.

I occasionally left a treat for him on my office credenza. Malcolm loved Clementine season. He'd never eaten a Minnesota-bred Haralson apple until I left one for him. *Too salty* he wrote of the empty V8 can he left on top of a handwritten thank you note.

Then I left him a candy bar.

Hershey's Extra Dark. Chocolate with sass. Serious Cacao.

I didn't know of Malcolm's allergic relationship with chocolate. He took offense. He thought I knew about his hypersensitivity. He interpreted my contribution as a racial slur, a reference to the deep coal tint to his skin, which I thought beautiful.

Post Candy Bar it didn't dawn on me how our paths ceased intersecting. When it did cross my mind I assumed he'd been reassigned. Malcolm had shared pieces of the inner workings of his custodial union. When a campus position opened it went out On Bid and was awarded to the person with the most seniority who requested it. I figured that's what happened. Malcolm got a better situation. I regretted missing a chance to say goodbye.

Turns out Malcolm asked for reassignment. I'd insulted him.

Of course I didn't hear this from Malcolm.

I heard it from Gayle Harte.

And here I am. Out of work, not entirely unhappy about my circumstances but heading home to a house located in a city I'd rather not live in. I have friends there. Kirkallen and Noir. I wonder what the heck I'm going to tell them. Let alone Heather.

Heather's the daughter who still talks to me.

FOUR

THE PATH TO BEAUTY

THE CHANCE TO WALK IN BEAUTY

"Congratulations!" Kirkallen exclaims when Hardy crosses his threshold. "It's the gift you've been dreaming about. And if you haven't been dreaming about it you should have. You have the chance to Walk in Beauty."

Muskie rushes to the door to greet Hardy and he pauses a moment to kneel and greet his faithful friend, a be-whiskered brindle mutt with a melting pot heritage. He endures her sloppy kisses and unlaces his practical Merrells and frets silently. *Is Kirkallen back on the sauce? What's with the beauty stuff?*

He knows Kirkallen is prone to odd declamation but the antecedents to this outbreak puzzle him. He stands.

"You find the key to the liquor cabinet? What in the name of Jesus are you spouting? Walking in beauty?"

"Duh. I sent you an email and I read your automatic reply. You no longer work at St. Rose. That's great news. The best I've heard in like forever."

"Oh … you know." Hardy breathes a sigh of relief. Kirkallen hasn't fallen off his supervised seat on the wagon.

"The provost's ghost writer wrote that," he says offhandedly. "I've resigned. Or am in the process of resigning."

26

Kirkallen is a wiry compact fellow. He wears khakis and an extra-large wool Pendleton he got for five bucks at the Goodwill. Lately he's slipped a woman's elasticized white garter around his left biceps.

He cuts to the chase. "You've hated your job for years. Did it for the paycheck and benefits. Tried like crazy not to smother under your own Baloney Slices. You never had the brass to cut the cord. Now you can walk the Beauty Way. Harmonize your life. Find your spiritual direction."

Remember the third chapter? Near the end you read about Kirkallen and his Navajo Phase?

This is it.

Though he's no expert Kirkallen knows more about the Beauty Way than your Narrator who writes here—but it doesn't take a genius to postulate that The Way leads to spiritual truth.

Noir emerges from the kitchen. Her sharp glance cuts through her elder friend. "Kirkallen told me."

She's prepared a classic movie line. This one Fred MacMurray directed at Barbara Stanwyck in *Double Indemnity*.

"'Do I laugh now, or wait 'til it gets funny?'"

Don't worry about Noir. That's not her name. You'll read her real one only once in this book though. The boys haven't called her *Caren Marie* in quite some time.

She lives with Hardy and Kirkallen and Muskie. She dresses *noir* when her Real Self is not demurely disguised by the professional garb she dons for her job in the St. Rose admissions office.

Kirkallen christened her after observing her predilection for off-hours attire, accompanied by her interest in Film Noir.

What you need to know immediately is the boys like Noir and she likes them. The boys especially like the latter fact. They like it she affectionately refers to them as *The Lads*.

Muskie? She's Hardy's dog but she loves Noir.

Noir continues to examine Hardy for fallout. "Best thing that could happen," she declares evenly. "Some jobs are stepping stones. Yours was a millstone. You kept it because you wanted to be near to what's left of your clan. Close to the one kid who talks to you. Close to your grandkids who love you. Even close to the artist who married your daughter."

Noir's not one to mince words. She's pretty much got Hardy pegged. He likes to believe she doesn't see through him. He's dreaming.

Hardy smiles and holds up his hands, palms out, playing traffic cop. "Whoa. Take it easy on a free man. Let me in the door first? Welcome me with *Hi* or *Good evening*? Better yet, *Supper's on the table*? At least Muskie came over to meet me."

"She wants a biscuit. We want the dope." Kirkallen is curious.

"Ditto," avers Noir.

She wears a denim apron over her work duds. A conservative charcoal skirt, a men's white button-down Oxford cuffed with Buffalo nickel links and a gray wool herringbone vest she snagged from Hardy's closet. In deference to her employment obligations she keeps her chestnut mane shoulder length. Occasionally she gathers it in a ponytail exposing a delicate alabaster neck.

As much as Noir downplays her feminine allure Kirkallen and Hardy see it and have the good sense to keep mum.

She possesses all the attributes straight men appreciate. A sturdy country frame, curves in the right places, legs that don't quit, enough shelf to support a cheek. Let's leave it there. Noir deserves better.

"As an appetizer," Hardy continues, "I'll tell you we're working on what Provost Harte terms *an Amicable Separation Agreement*."

"Hah," Kirkallen laughs, "you have two of those Amicable Deals going now. Abby and Gayle Harte."

Noir jumps in. "They're not in the same category, Kirky. I like Abby. I'm sorry she left Hardy. I'm sorry for their differences. The only good thing about their separation it is I get to live here. As for Harte? That chick's a ball buster. She has no heart. I could never work for her."

She thinks a moment, "Check that. I wouldn't work for her."

"I don't," Hardy replies.

It is a simple statement but the accompanying feeling is intense. An exhilarating rush courses through Hardy's frame.

He's free.

"I'm supposed to keep the negotiations confidential but I can tell you guys. You're Family. The short version is I'm a racist. A bigot. I'll explain over supper. Noir? You have anything going with that leftover salmon?"

"Supper's a work in progress," she asserts confidently.

"Kirkallen? Set the table? Maybe we step lightly off the wagon and open a nice Erath pinot? Go ultra-light on the Balvenie later?"

Hardy refers to the supervised nightcaps he sips with Kirkallen whose penchant for repeated and consistent over indulgence requires monitoring.

Noir pads toward the kitchen, a space she keeps in a neat and orderly fashion as opposed to the living areas cluttered with stray piles of books and magazines and papers, a fly-tying bench, a busy work desk and an assortment of fishing tackle.

The boys are happy to yield the cooking space to her. As is Muskie. Ever hopeful she trails steadfastly behind her soul mate. The young woman pivots and confronts the hound.

"Shame on you, bitch. I already fed you. All you want from me is a treat and you're using your female wiles, your hangdog look, to beg for more. You have no pride."

"Language," Kirkallen responds automatically. He enjoys playing the father he never got to be.

Noir is unable to resist editorializing.

"The description fits. Muskie is a literal bitch." A challenging gleam flashes in her dark eyes. "Gayle Harte is a metaphorical bitch."

"Touché," Kirkallen assents. "But that's beside the point. Basically I need to know more about the Racist Baloney Slices."

Baloney Slices. Part of Kirkallen's beauty walk is avoiding harsher words. Juxtapose the first letter of each word and you get his gist.

"The racist charge? It is a stretch," Hardy admits.

Kirkallen doesn't wish to sound flippant or disrespectful but he feels compelled to clarify, "Harte obviously doesn't know you played summer hoops for a team called the Soul Patrol Plus One."

❖

THE BEST NUANCE

Caren Marie Caruso sets down a tureen of salmon chowder, a mélange of Easter dinner leftovers and assorted refrigerated bits. Fingerling potatoes, a diced carrot and celery stalk, one finely chopped shallot, unmeasured dollops of heavy cream, thawed fish stock, a bay leaf, fresh-ground pepper, cut-up salmon steak.

Hardy serves spinach salads lightly coated with Noir's signature vinaigrette. Kirkallen engages a traditional jazz playlist on Spotify, plops down the napkins he neglected when he set the table and produces a warm baguette. Real butter.

"I biked to the co-op for the bread. Got my butt good and soaked on the ride home." He knows Noir loves their crusty loaves. He would willingly bike through Hell to bring it home for her.

"Friends." Hardy sits and extends his arms toward his compatriots, his adopted strays. The trio closes the circle by clasping hands.

Hardy eyes Noir. "Your turn."

She shrugs and regards her housemates. Odd men with big hearts. Men more than twice her age who allow her the space she needs and don't get creepy.

"I'm not a praying girl," she says shyly, "but I know this truth. 'Sometimes I wonder what strange fate brought me out of the storm to that house that stood alone in the shadows,' but here I am, living with you lads and I am more than grateful for this food and for our friendships."

"Amen," intones Hardy. They drop hands. "You got me on that one. What's it from?"

"Part comes from Bogey in *The Big Sleep*. The rest is mine."

"Please pour the wine?" Kirkallen asks.

"A glass." Hardy admonishes his friend.

"Two and I'm done."

"One and you're definitely done," Noir and Hardy state firmly.

They eat slowly and savor the vintage. They top off the meal with servings of whole bean vanilla ice cream drenched in warm Wisconsin maple syrup.

Hardy explains his day, finishing with Officer Erickson's private assessment of his former boss, even the comment about his desire to use the gym. The one item he consciously omits is the piece concerning young women in tights.

"To review," Noir swipes her mouth with a napkin, "you don't represent what you call *a testosterone threat* to a middle age chick when you get caught copping a peek at her boobs; you're insulted when you're told you have eighteen years left to live; you're the Invisible Man in the doctor's office; you experience a bumper sticker revelation at a snowy American intersection while listening to Jimmy Cliff; you provide an ornithology lesson for your ex-boss who then accuses you of being a racist but then you want to kiss the same lady you don't want to see naked?"

"Other than one correction I couldn't have stated it more succinctly but your summary does lack nuance."

"What's the correction?"

"I didn't take the Eighteen Years Comment as an insult. I heard it as a Wake-Up Call."

"I'll take that as a positive. But I do worry about you finding What's Next. I don't think that's a job so I'll refrain from quoting a Butch Cassidy line that could sprinkle a bit of angst on your nuance."

Kirkallen lifts his glass and taps his friends' goblets. "The best nuance is regardless of the bogus charge, our buddy gets to reinvent his life."

"Whoa. I feel nervous when you put that spin on it. Though I don't know exactly what I want down the road, what I need is for you guys to let me tell Heather, okay? I figure a daughter oughta hear news like this from her dad."

"If she emails and reads the automatic response?" Noir queries.

"I'll take that chance. She's beyond email. She's a Texting Girl Going Instagram. Whatever that is. If I need to reach her, I text."

Noir pushes away from the table and stands. She stares at Hardy.

"Since you're not working? I hope one thing."

"What?"

"I hope you don't move. I know you've always wanted to live in the country. You hate city living. I love living here. You hearing me on this? Am I being clear enough?" She strides toward the kitchen, Muskie trailing in her wake.

"Hey Noir?" Hardy calls.

"What?"

"I'm curious about the Butch Cassidy reference."

"'I'm too old to hunt up another job,'" she yells.

"And that's a blessing," Kirkallen affirms.

I ALWAYS FORGET THIS PART

Speaking of blessings, Kirkallen is a blessing in my life. You need to know about him. His story is complicated. I'll sketch a thumbnail here.

He hails from a Pennsylvania steel mill town where his father managed the plant. We met at the close of his undergraduate struggle. Fresh from flunking out of Rutgers, his third collegiate ejection, Kirkallen took my order at the Peacock Inn in Princeton. We bonded over after-hours drinks at the Inn bar and wound up living with other grad school stragglers in a rent-free abandoned Victorian on seminary property. Kirkallen introduced me to the Green Stuff and our friendship deepened.

Largely unable to complete what he started, the Rutgers experience completely severed his familial ties. It broke his mother's heart when her husband sent their son packing with the valediction *Come back when you're ready to be a man.*

Kirkallen commenced to do Manly Things.

He forged his own path through street drugs, alcohol, failed relationships and menial jobs. We gradually lost touch. Then an Ex called me out of the blue. She tearfully confessed to abandoning her redemptive efforts.

I found Kirkallen in Portland, Oregon, sleeping under the Burnside Bridge clutching a half empty bottle of rotgut rye.

I woke him and he punched me in the mouth. A terse reminder he once took boxing lessons at one of the fancy New England prep schools he attended.

We quickly cleared that hurdle.

I cleaned him up, brought him home and put a roof over his head, given the premise we'd share in monitoring the addictions that profoundly occupied his life.

I put him to work around the house and yard. He's a genius at fixing things and I have an old Suburban and rambling home. Each requires maintenance and repair. As you know, our snowblower starts first-time every-time. The Suburban does too.

Getting High gradually ceased being my friend's life's work. Together we're managing his addictions in an unusual but effective fashion.

Kirkallen knows he'll always be an alcoholic. Given that constant he goes through what he terms *My Phases*. You know he's currently preoccupied by All Things Navajo. He'll tell you he's doing his level best to walk the Beauty Way, prompted because he's reading a series of Tony Hillerman mysteries set in the desert southwest.

The author's a white guy with honorary tribal status. He dispenses lovely nuggets about the *Dineh* culture while producing intriguing mysteries. I like what Hillerman I've read. He makes me want to visit the Four Corners. At the moment I'm content to let Kirkallen tell me about the Hillerman I haven't read.

Kirkallen's as short as I am tall. He's worn his hair buzzed since I cut it off and tossed him into my Oregon hotel shower. His beard is tight and trimmed and pure white like his hair. His skin is beautiful. Remarkable since he spent a good deal of time on the street. His rich chocolate eyes peer out at you through oval metal frames. He's diet conscious but eats much better meals since Noir moved in. I do too.

He's lean and fit and follows an arcane martial arts workout regimen, which he augments with long bike rides on the multitude of Twin Cities trails.

He's loquacious. He never met a story he doesn't like. He tends toward telling epics. Sagas with subplots that make multiple detours. If he begins a tale in Saint Paul with Denver as an ultimate destination he's likely to travel via Nashville and Natchez to get there.

Oh. I always forget this part. I don't know why Kirkallen didn't mention it when we discussed the racist charges leveled against me. His rationale for obviating my racist tendencies took the form of a comment that I once played for a park league basketball team. The sole white guy on an otherwise all black team.

Kirkallen is African-American. Adopted shortly after birth by a childless Caucasian couple when Kirkallen's birth mother died unexpectedly and no one else willingly stepped in.

He's kept me sane.

I saved his life.

And Noir's doing her level best to save us.

SHE HEARD WE HOPED TO RENT OUR THIRD FLOOR?

We don't know much about Noir.

A few years ago she knocked on our door during my working day. Kirkallen answered and she presented as a freshly minted St. Rose graduate. She'd accepted the college's offer to work in Enrollment Management. She heard we hoped to rent our third floor?

We didn't. But that didn't stop Kirkallen.

He told her not to worry about the rent that we'd be cool. Which we are. Maybe she could cook once in a while, help with household chores?

She'd moved in by the time I got home.

We treat Noir like a daughter. It bugs me to think I treat her better than I treated Libby. We'll get to her as we move along.

As far as Noir's concerned Kirkallen and I have a Male Ego Thing going on. We are not recent inductees of the Invisible Male Association. We're card-carrying veterans. Younger women have looked *by* us for longer than they ever looked *at* us, thereby proving that young women are genetically wired *not* to see older men. Unless they have money.

Noir *sees* us. She legitimizes us.

We like that.

Noir's family now. She's threaded herself into the fabric of our lives. But other than her tendency toward incisive speaking and her love of film quotes, we know what you know.

Except she owns Italian ancestry. Great grandparents who lived in Parma and a grandmother who taught her to cook.

Except she lost her immediate family and the functional parts of her uterus in an unexplained accident.

The rest? When we ask she uses a standard response she quotes from *Lady in the Lake.*

"When it concerns a woman, does anyone really want the facts?"

Muskie's story is simpler.

She's a warm eyed, forty pound canine whose bedraggled ass I yanked from a fast moving trout river. That's all she needed to know. She snuck into the rear of my friend's pickup as we drove away from the river that day. We failed to notice until Alwin braked in front of my place. I don't know if Alwin's wife is allergic to dogs but it's what he said.

Muskie took up residence with Kirkallen and me. She's got a muskrat coat and a grease-gathering mustache, which I trim frequently. I tell her *A girl doesn't need a mustache.*

First night Noir stayed with us, Muskie slept at the foot of the girl's bed. I own Muskie but Noir owns Muskie's heart.

Kirkallen and I don't say it but we know Noir needs someone to love her. Muskie's a good place to start.

HARDY HOPES SHE DOESN'T LOSE IT

Five days hence Hardy inks his signature to a termination agreement guaranteeing three year's health insurance, a year's salary paid in a lump sum, an additional severance check and permission to use the school's fitness facilities.

He thinks it's a great deal.

The Peter, Paul & Mary song about the candy bar I mentioned earlier? There's a line in it the hippie utters in trying to explain his troubles as a result of his simple and genuine act of kindness.

"I only offered him a candy bar," the hippie says.

In this case Hardy's benevolence toward Malcolm proved troubling but he eventually reaped a huge reward. It's not supposed to work like that but it did.

On Friday the thirteenth he softly latches the door to Gayle Harte's suite behind him and quietly walks away from a peripatetic career in higher education without as much as a goodbye—and a check in his pocket.

He feels an enormous weight lift off his heart.

There's spring in his step when he walks home. For the first time in months he takes in his surroundings.

The snow has melted. Lilac buds are swelling. Maple sap pools on the sidewalk, drips down tree trunks. Daffodils bloom in bunches in the gardens he passes. Cardinals are what-cheering from the treetops. He wonders idly about the current moon phase, what planets he might see from his front porch. An eagle swoops low on its flight to the river, black wings glinting deep purple.

Alfred Lord Tennyson wrote of spring as a time when "a young man's fancy lightly turns to thoughts of love." In Hardy's case it's true.

He loves fly-fishing.

And the early season is rounding into shape.

He considers his new-found freedom. Maybe he can travel west and fish the Madison's storied Salmon Fly Hatch. He'd love to float hopper imitations over big Missouri River rainbows. The prospects are appealing. For the moment he grins and forms the day's mental game plan.

Pack his gear and go fish the Kinni. He might run into a Blue-winged Olive hatch, one of Hardy's very favorite river events.

He picks up his pace and strides more briskly toward his oversized frame home. One he purchased on whim after making a casual offer on an upcoming estate sale.

His daughter's Mercedes sedan is parked out front. Her work car.

Talking with Heather will cancel his fishing plans. Hardy hopes she doesn't lose it when he tells her he's out of work.

Hardy's about to discover the First Rule about Not Working. It debunks the myth perpetrated by the Working Slobs. They think people who don't work can do what they want when they want.

They can't. And don't.

FUNNY HOW THAT WORKS

You're about to meet my daughter but first there's one thing I forgot to say about Noir, something you probably know but I want to make sure you do.

Kirkallen and I love her.

It's something we know but don't tell her. We don't even admit it to each other. But we do love her in spite of the fact we don't like that she sees through us, reads us like open books, tells us when we we're off base and when we're full of it or downright lying to ourselves. It does feel a trifle unsettling when a brash mid-twenties woman speaks as accurately and forthrightly about our foibles and weaknesses—but there you have it.

Maybe it's because she's female. Women are much smarter than us guys.

Remember Noir's initial reaction to the news of My Resignation? She described my job as a *millstone*? She cut to the chase and told me I kept the job as a security blanket and as an excuse to stay close to Heather and her family? Then she said she hoped Kirkallen and I don't move to the country?

She's spot on. And her first premise is patently obvious.

My job was a millstone.

Noir's next two assertions could use some explaining. I'll mix them together here.

A recent issue of *Minnesota Monthly* magazine featured an article about *the best of city living*. That's an oxymoron as far as I'm concerned.

I prefer rustic byways to city boulevards. I like open spaces and quiet places. I never thought I'd end up living in a city. Though we live in a peaceful neighborhood I despise hearing the Interstate Hum and the frequent blare of sirens. I also enjoy a legit chance to see the night sky. Here in town it takes an especially clear evening to locate the North Star.

Put in perspective I'd love to move but my family connections are here. Heather and Kyle and the girls. I love them. And Noir's right. Heather's my only immediate family member who talks to me.

Then there's the house Abby and I own. Then there's Kirkallen and Noir.

Talk about anchors. I'm not going anywhere.

Bottom line? People do weird things in the name of love.

I'm surprised. It turns out the Family and Location Thing is much easier to explain than I thought. I'm discovering a novel concept. Things become clearer when you put thoughts and feelings into words. Funny how that works.

Food for thought.

I'll bear that in mind as I hand this chronicle over to our Narrator. You're about to meet Heather and I'm not sure I can handle dealing with her in the first person quite yet. I've had enough Emotional Discourse for one day.

I HAVE A GOOD IDEA FOR STARTERS

Micah Hardy walks away from his job and toward a new life. He bounds up his front steps, grabs the mail and pushes the door open.

"Daddy, you're smiling. You took the porch steps in one go. You look younger." Heather hugs her dad.

Always physically demonstrative Heather used her healthy six-two frame in the high school low post and as a walk-on who earned regular minutes at the University of San Diego.

Hardy returns her hug. Tight. He clinches for several seconds and recalls wistfully how he held a much younger and smaller Heather.

He releases his daughter and summons the energy to explain his resignation in the face of her anticipated concern. He bends to greet the ever devoted Muskie. Heather leaves space for him to speak. The air is redolent with the scent of a freshly baked apple pie.

He delivers the simple facts as he sorts bills from the chaff of postal aggregate, recycling the majority of it.

"Like you think I didn't know? We are family and we talk ... word gets around."

"You're saying I've fretted about telling you news you knew?"

Heather ignores the comment. "It's about time. You never liked your job. You sold yourself short doing it. St. Rose took advantage of you and they reduced you. Shrunk your spirit. For the last couple of years your idea of a good time consisted of watching food and travel shows and hoping Giada would bend over the salad far enough to give you an eyeful."

Kirkallen strides into the living room. "Speaking of eyefuls, it's probably best you don't know much more about what goes on in a man's mind. You might take offense to know our thinking."

Heather swivels to face Kirkallen whom she treats as a beloved uncle. "I believe you're operating under a false assumption, dear."

"'It's happened," Kirkallen allows.

"You assume men have minds. That they think."

Hardy ignores the banter. "There's a back story to my leaving. Do you know that too?"

Heather shakes her head.

"Then perhaps my friend would like to elucidate?" Hardy knows his companion loves a monologue.

Kirkallen begins outlining the details and Heather realizes she's in for a Verbal Sunday Drive. She beckons the pair toward the kitchen with a toss of her dark blonde locks, which she keeps long per Kyle's preference. "How about I serve up some pie and coffee while we hear this back story?"

The summary lasts ten times longer than Noir's succinct post-dinner recap but embraces the finer points, including Adele's cleavage, the Jimmy Cliff and bumper sticker and eighteen years revelations, the repartee in the Provost's office and, naturally, the main course concerning Malcolm and the Candy Bar.

The bronze skinned man closes his summary. "So … basically … basically your dad's a racist."

"We all are on some level," Heather says matter-of-factly.

"True. But I'm thinking Ms. Harte doesn't know an African-American is your dad's best friend. His resignation …"

"Is voluntary." Hardy interjects. "The agreement I signed today mentions no allegations."

Kirkallen concludes, "So your dad's a free man. As far as I can see it's all good, We can go fishing and that Harte bitch can kiss my …"

Hardy interrupts the lean diminutive man. "No Negative Waves. Remember you're trying to Walk in Beauty?"

Heather regards the confrontational pair.

Friends joined at the hip. Older men tuned to an identical frequency. She's pleased her father keeps his friend sober and understands the friend's frankness rescues her dad from self-absorption. She knows Noir keeps them in line.

Though Heather considers Noir an Exotic Species she and Noir are bonded through a fast friendship and their mutual love—and sisterly concerns—for their boys. Heather misses her mom, regrets her abrupt departure, for which she feels a tinge of unnecessary guilt, but she is delighted Noir has converted the Pair into a Trio.

Heather Hardy Bartlett chews and swallows a last bite of pie. "Kyle and the girls hope you'll come over for supper tonight. They want to celebrate."

Olivia and Amelia. Kyle and Heather's teenagers.

As she removes the dishes Hardy catches his daughter in profile and sees his wife. It pops out of his mouth unbidden.

"You're lucky you got your mama's looks, girl."

In the ensuing silence a catalog of personal failures flickers on Hardy's mental videotape. Principally among them the confrontation he created with college-age Elizabeth when he arrived home much earlier than anticipated during a New Year's Eve ice storm and saw more of his daughter than he'd seen since last changing her diapers. He didn't ask for an explanation. He booted the guy and refused to apologize. Libby never returned after she left for the spring semester.

Then when Heather married and moved out Abby left too. She claimed she couldn't live with Hardy anymore.

The man who chased away their younger child.

The man who didn't attend church or much less believe in it—or God—for that matter.

Hardy's not quite sure where that came from but he's living with it. We'll sort through these issues in due time.

Heather sighs. "Mom's living Up North and working with the Sisters. She gets caught up in her causes. We haven't heard from her lately. My girls don't get it. They wish she'd keep better touch but cell service is ridiculous up there."

"Ridiculous cell service? What an appealing concept. One your girls would never get." Kirkallen wiggles his snowy eyebrows. He loves Heather's daughters. They love him.

Heather fondly eyes the wiry brown man. "Mom leaves and we get you."

"At least I'm glad to be here." He spreads his arms. "Your dad saved my life."

"And I'm glad you pair of hopeless cases have Noir." Heather totes the dishes to the sink. Muskie trails hopefully behind.

"So are you boys coming to supper?" Hardy's daughter asks. "Noir too, if she's not busy."

Her back's to her father and she's washing and stacking dishes. She turns off the water, dries her hands on her skirt and states quietly, "After supper we need to help Dad figure out what he's going to do with his life. I have a good idea for starters."

Hardy rolls his eyes.

Kirkallen guffaws. "This should be rich," he says.

"Jesus," Hardy mutters and shakes his head. "I can't wait."

THINKING OUT LOUD

You probably want to know about Abby and the Religion Thing. In the third chapter you discovered she left me because she said I didn't Believe Right. You've just heard more about our split. I should try to clarify.

What Abby calls my Failure to Believe I call Healthy Questioning.

Maybe I blew it when I thought out loud with her. I thought she'd appreciate me sharing my questioning God and the church with her.

I told her I struggled to believe. I said something like if God exists and is All Powerful he's doing a terrible job of managing Things Here on Earth since everywhere you look we're making a mess of it.

I suggested He might be a practical joker. Having a good laugh on the humans He created, seeing how miserable we can be. I tried to soften it by saying God had to be a He. A woman would never do such a poor job at creation.

That didn't help much but at least Abby smiled.

I also told my wife I struggled with Christianity's exclusivity. I cited a verse from John's gospel. Something written more than fifty years after Jesus died. John puts words in his Savior's mouth in the fourteenth chapter. Depending on which translation you choose it sounds something like this. "No man comes to the Father but by me."

I told Abby I couldn't imagine a god so small-minded as to disregard all the other peoples on our planet, let alone one whole gender.

John's Christianity sounds country-clubbish. Like a religion for a people living in a gated community. I said I didn't think Jesus would want to live in a place like that. I'd like to think the Lord would want to be more inclusive.

I thought I did my part though. I stood on the altar of the Church of the Ascension for our kids' baptisms. I vowed to rear them in the Catholic Tradition. And we did. We sent the girls to parochial schools and paid out the wazoo for the privilege. I did all the proper parent-things. We did the First Communion and the Confirmation gigs. I took the kids to church regularly but I admit Masses felt tedious. Yeah I concede I stopped going after the girls left home.

Truth told my church doesn't have walls. It's a trout stream. Good on me for not saying that out loud.

Even though I kept my word, after the girls left home Abby got super-involved with her faith and the church—ladies' do-good committees, a prayer group, bake sales, a sewing circle, Bible study sessions and trips to the nursing home to take communion to shut-ins.

I couldn't do it. It felt dishonest. I couldn't hide my ambivalence.

Bottom line? I did not match my wife's zeal but it came as a total surprise, a shot out of the blue, when she said I didn't Believe Right and split. I've not been the same since.

After telling you this? Hearing it again?

I blew it.

I think my Healthy Questioning probably came across as Criticism. As criticizing Abby.

I didn't mean it to sound that way. I'm sorry if it did. I should've kept my mouth shut. Should've realized what most husbands instinctively know. They must deliberately and thoughtfully filter what they share honestly with their wives.

Look where thinking out loud got me.

Thinking out loud with Abby put my butt in a sling.

WHAT A GOOD FATHER WOULD DO

I took Heather aside prior to supper and told her to go easy on the What Are You Going to Do with Your Life routine. We needed to work our plan gently and not force it. She promised she would but she's pressing too hard now.

We've finished supper. Olivia and Amelia have cleared the table and are in the kitchen brewing coffee and slicing dessert. They're doing it as quickly as they can. They want to hear what's happening.

I don't blame them.

They'd see their mom talking *about* her dad. Not *to* him. Like he's not there, as if he's a Third Party we're subjecting to academic scrutiny.

This is Noir. You've read enough about me to form an opinion but you haven't heard from me. I'll jump in here because I have a hunch I'm going to play a larger role in the proceedings than planned. For one thing the Narrator likes me. Probably more than he should. He's linked me with Heather and her friends to keep me involved. You'll meet the friends if you keep reading.

I've gotten to know Abby and her daughters and her good friend Hannah. I've even met Hannah's daughter. She's nice. For a minister. I'm not sure what to make of that.

I don't expect to talk much. I'm an extremely private person. I carry a load of hurt. Like Hardy I'm terrible at sharing. To be more clear?

I can be a bitch.

I refuse to discuss My Personals with all but a very few.

The *few*? We're either not talking. Or they're dead.

That's why I like The Lads. They accept me without making judgments. They don't pry. Never ask for more than I'm willing to tell.

My gender's also a non-issue with them. Age difference helps. They treat me like a daughter. Except they don't try to control me. Which they know they shouldn't. And can't. Which is good.

And they are guys. Once in a while I catch them sneaking a peek down my shirt. We're talking normal behavior.

I'm sure you've figured out The Lads are more than a little important to me but I should back up.

St. Rose has been good to me. I'm not even Catholic but the school paid for my education on account of My Circumstances. After graduation I felt I owed them when they offered me a job. I had no real plans, plus facing an Unknown Future intimidated me.

I accepted.

My housing search started and ended after having tea with a nun who taught me at St. Rose. She knew Kirky and suspected he'd be a soft touch. She said he and Hardy were harmless. She gave me the line to use. The one how I heard they were looking to rent their third floor. She told me where they lived and I went right over.

The moment Kirky opened the door we connected. We each sensed deep hurt in the other.

I remember thinking *I don't need to play the Cute Girl Card.* I gave him one line and room to talk. I knew he'd say *Yes.*

You already know it worked.

Four years later Hardy and Kirky know for sure I needed time, space and place. You could say I've blossomed. With their help. Heather's too.

At this moment however it's Hardy who needs time and space more than me.

Heather's pressing pretty hard on the What Are You Going to Do with Your Life Pedal. Kyle's giving her the Ease Up Eye. She's not reading it.

Poor Hardy. He just left a job he disliked immensely. He's tasting freedom for the first time but he feels a need to account for himself. He's squirming in his seat like a grammar school kid. Someone needs to intervene.

It's me.

Fortunately I can say things to Heather her father can't. "What do you say we break for dessert?"

I motion Heather toward the kitchen. "Why don't you see how the girls are doing? I think your dad needs room to breathe. He's got time to form a Game Plan for his new life. I'm not even sure he needs one. What he needs is to go fishing."

Heather takes my not-so-subtle hint. She realizes she's forgotten our game plan. The one we worked out yesterday morning over a pot of Darjeeling. Like you think it was a coincidence Heather was baking a pie when Hardy got home from his last day at work?

Heather rises. "Another Indeed, Daddy?" she asks.

"I like their pale ale. Day Tripper." Kyle's trying to break the tension too.

Hardy nods his assent.

Kirkallen's also attempting to pour oil on troubled waters. "Day Tripper. An excellent name for a beer." He considers the name. "That used to be me."

"I'll fetch a Kaliber for you, Mr. Kirkallen." Heather heads toward the kitchen.

Kyle stocks the non-alcoholic beverage for Kirky's visits but he's seriously into craft beers. He can sound as pedantic as the snootiest of oenologists. I pose a question to wind him up.

Ten minutes later we've talked malt and mouthfeel and hop-forward beers and new breweries and we're back on an even keel eating chocolate cake and sipping at coffee and beers.

Heather apologizes for her overbearing expression of concern. "Daddy," she modifies her tone, "I love you. I'm acting more worried than I feel ... that's all."

Heather can be a good liar when she needs to. She's not a woman for nothing.

As she continues her contrite apology I know her well enough to know she's using the Back Door Approach. She's softening him up. Reverting somewhat to her teenage self. It sounds like she's using a voice she might have used at sixteen.

To get what she wants.

She's circling the Good Idea she mentioned at supper. The Good Idea we talked about over tea.

The one where Hardy agrees to go to the wedding.

"You do need time, Daddy," Heather begins, "I shouldn't have pushed like I did. I shouldn't expect you to have any kind of definitive answer. You've got time. In fact you ought to take time and travel."

Hardy confesses, "There are hatches I've always wanted to fish. Salmon Flies and Green Drakes out west."

Like we didn't know?

"I have a great idea as far as travel goes."

Everyone's eyes fix on Heather.

"We're driving north in June. We're going to a wedding. Daddy, you ought to come with us. It's going to be outdoors. There'll be a party afterward. It's a chance to escape the city. Then you can stay on and fish some trout streams that drain into Superior. I've read the DNR stocks lakes with trout too."

"Who's getting married?" Hardy asks. "Wouldn't I need an invitation?"

"I think you could get one. You'll be family. You know Libby? Elizabeth Hardy? Your daughter? The one you haven't spoken to in like forever? It's her wedding."

It's the line I've been waiting for.

"You have to go," I say quickly. Then I deliver the clincher. The Guilt Trip Line. "It's what a Good Father would do …"

The sentence hangs there.

Wow.

Heather and I broadsided Hardy.

He's wearing a vacant shell shocked expression. He shocks us even more when he says, "Okay."

"Great," Heather quickly inserts. "I'll hold you to it. It'll be good for you. Good for Libby. Good for me too. I can get out of the middle of having to tell Libby about you and telling you about Libby. That'll be a relief. And since you and Mom will be in the same place, maybe you guys can actually talk to each other."

Heather doesn't want to go too far down that Abby Road. She breaks the mood with, "More coffee or beer anyone?"

Everyone opts for coffee and Olivia and Amelia serve it.

Over second cups we learn Libby's marrying someone named Alex at a mansion built by an early twentieth century lumber baron.

"They call the place *The House on the Hill*," Heather says as she sketches some details.

"Sounds cool," I interject as I place my hand possessively over Kirkallen's. "We can't wait. It'll be a blast."

No one flinches when I include myself and Kirkallen in the mix. To underscore our connections I throw in a quote Bacall used on Bogey in *Dark Passage*, changing it slightly from singular to plural.

"We've sort of joined your team."

I squeeze Kirky's hand. He squeezes back.

THEIR REGULAR NIGHTCAP

Kirkallen and Hardy sit bundled up on a brisk April evening and savor their regular nightcap. They lounge on the porch in a pair of creaky wicker chairs Hardy rescued from a barn loft. The Minnesota air is relinquishing its wintry bite but the boys' exhalations drift visibly away on the soft breeze.

It's an unusually clear evening. The pair peers through the bones of a front yard sugar maple. They regard the heavens they understand they're fortunate to see. Orion is completing his late winter hunt across the southern sky. His principal stars—Betelgeuse and Rigel—are disappearing into the filigree of an urban tree line.

The men grip exquisitely cut Galway crystal tumblers that glisten, reflecting the street light, and appreciatively swish the amber liquid inside. Balvenie Caribbean Cask.

Neither can truly afford the price of the Speyside scotch, matured fourteen years in oak barrels and finished in casks formerly containing Caribbean rum. But they consume mere thimblefuls in the course of their evening ritual. Hardy dispenses it judiciously, a mini-fix for his addicted friend. He returns the bottle to a cupboard he secures with a key.

Kirkallen raises his glass. "Water of Life," he utters reverently.

He sips and completes his thought. "When the docs give me the Terminal Diagnosis? I'm jumping seriously off the wagon and into the malts and barleys."

"We'll jump off that bridge when we come to it," Hardy replies evenly.

The elderly pair retreats to communal taciturnity as a car whooshes by.

Hardy cannot completely relax. The prospect of Libby's Impending Nuptials has him at Sixes and Sevens.

"What was I thinking? I have to be out of my mind to agree to go to the wedding. I think I said *Yes* to get Heather and Noir off my back. You think Libby's gonna be happy to see me? Turn cartwheels?"

Hardy winces at a mental image of his leggy primary-age daughter to whom he taught the gymnastic maneuver.

For once Kirkallen fails to respond.

"I mean I'm not against trying to reconcile but maybe her wedding isn't the greatest timing. I don't want to screw up her day. Plus the guy's family is bound to think I'm some kind of weirdo. Reappearing after all this time?"

"They won't be too far off on the weirdo part will they?" Kirkallen deadpans.

"Jesus," Hardy says, "you're a help."

Kirkallen begins, "Look at it like this. Why not see if you can make things right with Libby? Break the ice with a simple *I'm sorry* and a promise to talk when the time is right. It's your chance to Walk in Beauty. No sense in hanging on to Negative Bygones. That's not healthy."

"You and your *Dineh* mumbo jumbo," Hardy snorts.

"How about trying this radical approach? Think of it as a fun time. We're going to a celebration at a lumber baron's fancy mansion built on a hill above a historic harbor town. There's no church ceremony involved. That's a plus. The wedding's outdoors and will probably be conducted by a renegade lady minister who'll wear a purple dress. Maybe she'll be cute. There'll be live music; probably dancing and decent eats. If things get too weird we can always go fishing. And I'm saving the best for last."

Kirkallen halts his description and sips his Balvenie.

"The best?" Hardy prompts.

"Your Ex will be there. You guys need to talk. It's a great opportunity to make a bunch of things right at the same time. While you're enjoying the wedding and getting on an even keel with Libby you can also work out what you and Abby want to do."

"I can't quite envision the Great Opportunity you're describing," Hardy retorts. "Besides Abby's not my Ex. We'd have to talk more to make divorce happen and she's not. At least not to me. She's mentioned the Amicable Separation deal but she's too busy with her Cause of the Month. Heather keeps telling me about them but I can't keep them straight. The current one has something to do with saving a dying convent."

"Well … maybe your lady doesn't sleep in your rack anymore but she's got a big heart."

"Abby has found her causes lately," Hardy comments. "I'll say this. It sounds like she's going after it Big Time. Good for her."

Kirkallen slides closer to the porch rail and kicks his feet up. He readjusts the white armband he's worn since The Election. "You won't have to worry about one thing," he says.

"What thing?"

"Me. I'll be keeping my nose out of the punch bowl. Noir and I talked when we returned from supper. She'll be my date. I'll be her escort. Guaranteed she'll keep her eye on me. We can trust that girl."

Hardy agrees. "That we can."

"She's the Daughter You Took In after the Other One left. Now it's time to get the Other One back."

"What are you? A psychologist?"

"A backhanded one," Kirkallen admits. "I don't have a license. What I got is Streetwise Smarts."

MAYBE SHE CAN HELP

As Part Four concludes I'm betting you find it ironic I got in Dutch with Abby because I didn't Believe Right. Mostly because I'm skeptical about Jesus being The Only Way to Salvation, that I can't imagine such a small-minded god. And yet I've called his name no fewer than six times already. You've heard me. I've also described Gayle Harte's appearance as *God-given*. I told Malcolm I wished my faith was as strong as his. Doesn't that strike you as odd?

I'm asking you to bear with me. I'll keep making Christian, if not religious, references when I talk. But I'm curious to know more about it.

You got any ideas?

Am I trying to believe? Or am I simply making habitual and cultural White America references? How to figure?

What do you say we head up to The House on the Hill? See if we can make any sense of it? We're going to a wedding. Kirkallen says there'll probably be a lady minister there. Maybe she can help.

Regardless, I'm thinking I'm in for an adventure.

FIVE

THE HOUSE ON THE HILL

A WOODEN EMPIRE

It's my responsibility to describe the basic wedding tableau, to tell you where we're going. I've served as the most descriptive narrator thus far. I've told you about the weather, the natural setting, how people look and what they're wearing. Which is why the first section of this enterprise is titled *mis-en-scène*. I'm trying to create the story board for the remainder of the narrative cast. It's my responsibility to provide a context to help you understand the characters' internal and external conversations. It is possible you'll get some description from Hardy after he starts partaking again and arrives at the lake. He's got a bit of poet in him. But it is only fair to advise you that I am losing control over the cast. They're speaking on their own accord. There's a kind of magic in that.

This is your Narrator again. We're headed to The House on the Hill. I know more about its history than anyone because I invented it. I'll tell you about it. Plus the area's too beautiful not to mention. I'll bring the landscape into focus too.

Cedar Harbor is a Lake Superior inlet fed by a river with the identic riverine name. It's a naturally formed cove, ringed by groves of ancient cedar and lined with basalt. Lava that solidified after spilling out of a colossal rift in earth's crust and spreading over pre-Cambrian bedrock nearly two billion years old.

Rock from a time before time.

A deep concept.

Robert Kerr arrived at a rugged and rustic outpost there in the late 1800s. The son of a Scot-Irish immigrant immediately took to the place.

How could he not? Scots are genetically wired to love Hard Land.

He marveled at the sheer open sky, how it covered such a vast expanse of water, the clouds and lake perpetually alive and active. He recognized the land's promise. He saw Opportunity when he considered the densely forested interior. He decided to make his fortune from the region's most obvious and obtainable resource.

Timber.

Kerr built a wooden empire. A lumber industry and a sawmill. He harvested acres of red pine. Towering trees over a hundred years old, the straight grain well suited for building. The first cut yielded enough telegraph poles to string telegraph line from the St. Croix River to the western Minnesota border.

The perspicacious man milled hundreds of thousands of board feet of timber, converting it into hard green cash.

He seldom made a political or financial move without purpose. He invested judiciously in Cedar Harbor's infrastructure, earning a reputation as a popular benefactor, a regard he occasionally underscored by buying a round for the house at the town watering hole.

He induced a young physician to settle, fulfilling a desperate medical need. Because he desired more sophisticated instruction for his two daughters he imported a Wellesley-educated schoolmarm. He founded a modest library.

The devout Presbyterian visited Princeton Theological Seminary and returned with a young pastor in tow for whom he built a church to preach in and a manse to live in. To showcase his ecumenical attitude he provided the lumber and the workforce when a group of renegade Catholic sisters asked him to build a convent and chapel beyond the edge of town.

Even Presbyterians find it difficult to say *No* to a group of polite persistent nuns garbed in full habit.

Locals thought the foresighted man a trifle odd. Kerr walked briskly about town, describing in detail to inquirers the benefits of vigorous pacing and of breathing lake air. His mind seldom rested. He thought aloud as he wandered. He uttered pithy phrases and from time to time stopped to jot notes on blank cards he kept in a vest pocket for that purpose. A visible citizen as he moved among home, offices, warehouses—or in the saddle when he rode out to job sites—Kerr established himself as the town's preeminent persona, a City Father.

His industry brought work and commerce and new blood to Cedar Harbor. Aside from the ancillary businesses necessitated by the lumber trade, fishermen began to settle and probe the lake for herring. Settlement became hamlet, hamlet became village as Kerr's bank account swelled.

A man of vision, Kerr erected an unusual and outsized manor on a hill overlooking the harbor. He could afford to Build Big. He owned the lumber. He shingled his residence with cedar.

From the town below the homestead loomed obviously, but not ostentatiously, above it. Folks took to calling it *The House on the Hill*. They called Robert *Baron*, a respectful reference to his business acumen and generous spirit.

To Robert's everlasting regret his and Margaret's first-born child, a son, refused to learn the business. Ross abhorred the Isolated Life. He despised the winter weather, the summer insects and all that sawdust.

The strong-minded young man mirrored his father's drive and determination. But the stubborn son proved more stubborn than his progenitor. He wanted to establish a separate identity. Over his father's objections he left to seek his fortune and subsequently enlisted when American troops mustered for World War I.

He never returned to Cedar Harbor. He moved to a more temperate clime after decommission.

He settled in North Carolina where he opened a moving and hauling business, becoming a successful entrepreneur in his own right.

When Ross departed, his Scot-proud daddy refused to utter the son's name, He began treating his daughters as sons. They willingly studied the lumber business and gladly accepted their father's offer to fund their college educations.

Back East of course.

A careful man and a thoughtful planner, Robert didn't plan on dying prematurely. He succumbed to the influenza pandemic, leaving his wife and young-twenties daughters in charge of Kerr Forest Products.

Leah and Rachel, recent college graduates christened with Biblically inspired names, had come home to live while they schemed over the shape and direction of their maturing years. As young women with modern attitudes they desired richer fuller lives than mores condoned.

With their father gone they looked no further.

More than familiar with the business, they donned wool trousers and denim work shirts and heavy boots and bunched their locks under bandanas and scarves and brimmed work hats. They frequented the saw mill and the harvest sites, rode with drayers as horses hauled downed timber to the mill. They shadowed foremen and mastered every aspect of the lumber trade from the inside out. Each determinedly held her own when gripping one handle of a bucksaw, pushing and pulling in tandem with a man.

At the close of their working days they removed their clothes in the mud room, shook the saw dust from their hair, donned dresses and savored drams of their father's best spirits on the front porch.

The siblings traveled to Duluth and the Twin Cities, to Milwaukee and Chicago—and points in between—to secure contracts. They skillfully conducted business in board rooms and with town councils and embraced their father's beneficent public attitude. They carved their rightful niches as influential businesswomen in a Man's World.

They thought radical thoughts.

They planted where they'd harvested.

They stood first in line to cast votes after the Suffrage Amendment passed.

They supported Margaret Sanger and her American Birth Control League.

They smoked the occasional cigar.

You know they'd taken a liking to their father's stash of malt spirits.

Far from unattractive, they fended off suitors. Some claimed they favored their own gender. Some believed they put more than tobacco in their cigars. But not many knew for sure.

Those who knew kept mum.

As time passed, they nursed their mother through age-related infirmities and interred her remains next to her husband's in a plot near The House, a cedar grove overlooking the Big Lake. Since Margaret so loved The House on the Hill—the stained glass, corner towers, columned porches and balconies—Leah and Rachel demurred when a stonecutter recommended *Gone Home* as an appropriate inscription.

They directed him to etch *At Home, At Peace* on their mother's marker.

The women aged and they sold the business, retiring with substantial funds to watch from the front porch of The House on the Hill as the world changed with increasing and alarming velocity even as they continued to fund area projects and charities. When they expired, and they did within a month of each other, the Town Council buried them next to their mother and father. No one came forward to claim the property and it gradually fell into disrepair.

There are those who find a certain magic in the Mystical North Country. They claim spirits wander in the night—abroad in the rough country, on the lakes and streams and byways, even in certain hallways. Some claim the spirits of Leah and Rachel occasionally ramble after the sun sets. Not many see them.

Muskie will.

WHAT'S ALL THE FUSS?

It's June. Kirkallen and Noir and I are driving toward The House on the Hill. We have no idea what we're getting into but we're going and we're psyched.

I'm surprised I'm looking forward to seeing Libby and meeting Her Guy.

Nervous? Sure.

But eager.

That's what two months of trout fishing can do for you. So yeah I've wrapped my mind around this Wedding Prospect. I'm also down with seeing Abby too.

Heather and Noir haven't said much about the wedding or Libby's intended. We know nothing about the ceremony. Zip about the ensuing celebration or even where we're staying. Except at a cottage on the property.

This is what Heather said. *No need to dress formal. Look presentable and pack for several days.*

This is what Noir said. *You lads better be on your best behavior.*

Noir's in her off-duty clothes—formfitting black jeans, blackened lashes, black lipstick, shiny black ear posts, high red Converse sneakers and a contour hugging black tee we made her cover with a long sleeve fishing polo we had in the car.

"Too distracting," Kirkallen admonished.

She's driving what she calls her *Establishment Car*. A Forester she managed to buy largely because she lives rent-free with her lads.

That's us.

Kirkallen tells me more progressive Minnesotans call the Subaru a *Lesbian Car.*

I don't get it.

No surprise there.

We're traveling together because we want to. Kirkallen and I prefer not to drive. We'd rather get lit and enjoy the scenery.

In inventing my New Life I've taken up an old habit. After forty-plus years of Not Indulging, mostly because of being a husband to Abby and a father to my girls, I'm glad I'm toking again.

I love a good buzz.

The stuff you get these days? It can be lethal. But there is an upside. All you need is one miniscule hit. Like my fishing friend Alwin says about dubbing a trout fly, *Less is more.*

We're also driving with Noir because my granddaughters begged to drive my Suburban. It's got a couple hundred thousand miles on it. The AC's long gone. One window motor's done. The roof is pocked with rust.

But the car runs like a top. Kirkallen's seen to that.

The girls claimed they needed their own wheels as an escape hatch in case things get too boring. Their anxious feelings are heightened by the prospect of venturing into Sketchy Cell and Wi-Fi Territory.

I outfitted the truck with new tires and filled the tank before handing over the keys. I told them no drinking and driving.

They looked at me like they'd look at some kind of clueless grandfather.

We're after stopping at a lakeside pullout so Noir and Muskie can sneak into the bushes and squat and so Kirkallen can work the kinks out by doing a piece of his flexibility regimen. We told him he couldn't take his mountain bike off the rear rack for a short pedal. We needed to take a stab at making decent time.

We also took the opportunity to light up. We're pleasantly buzzed, vibrating to Noir's Pink Martini iPhone playlist. She's plugged it into the car and somehow it plays through the speakers. Good stuff. There is something to be said for Modern Technology. Though not much.

The world is a beautiful place when viewed through polarized lenses. It's fresh, newly minted, especially when you're stoned.

The wind's up on the lake and the wave patterns are a source of endless fascination. Breakers crash and froth violently against antediluvian rock.

"I know wind when I see it," Noir says absently.

"Where'd that come from?" one of us asks.

She's wandered into her movie quote compendium. As far as we're concerned Noir's like one of those outrageously steep mountain climbs in the Tour de France. The ones called *hors catégorie*. She's beyond categorization.

"*The Old Dark House*. Boris Karloff. Melvyn Douglas. Charles Laughton."

"Oh."

We're steering back into spring as we gain latitude. The canopy's not quite filled out. Early spring wildflowers line the roads. Forest floors are rife with blooming anemone. The creeks are swollen with runoff.

"Too high and muddy to fish," Kirkallen remarks.

"But there're trout lakes where we're headed. I hope there's a canoe we can use."

"You boys and your fly rods," Noir comments. "Freud would say they're a substitute for a certain piece of the male anatomy. Maybe one that's not getting as much use at its owner wants." She affectionately scratches Muskie's skull.

Muskie's riding shotgun. We're in back. I'm sitting behind the hound. Her seat's pulled forward so I can stretch my legs.

"We are," Kirkallen explains, "Men of a Certain Age. That's one reason why we like an occasional toke. To keep us even. It's good for our *hozro.*"

Pink Martini plays on. Noir and I remain quiet.

"*Hozro?*" she finally asks.

"It's Navajo for describing a harmonious state of mind, for finding peace with your circumstances, for seeing the beauty in each day and in each person. It's a very essential component of the Navajo world view. And right this minute I'm feeling very *hozro*-like."

Kirkallen's gone overboard with his Navajo Phase lately.

Tony Hillerman wrote more than a dozen books and Kirkallen's reading them all. He says he's almost finished with the series and it's possible he's about to switch muses. He's carrying *The Pocket Pema Chodrön* in his chest pocket. He claims it's written by a woman who teaches Tibetan Buddhism at a Nova Scotia monastery. I can't wait for that.

A twelve-wheeler burns past at speed, its tires vibrating loudly at eye level. "I understand why dogs chase tires," Kirkallen says.

At the Cedar Harbor outskirts we pass a well-kept but aging hotel-like building. A four-story wood-frame structure set back from the road. It's nestled into budding maples and birch and aspen about halfway up the side of the Sawtooth ridge. A small chapel sits adjacent to the building. It positively gleams white. A permanent sign near the driveway entrance reads *The Convent of the Holy Sisters.*

A gaggle of placards populates the spacious front lawn.

Save The Convent.

DSG Go Home.

"What's all the fuss?" Kirkallen comments idly.

"I'm thinking they'll tell us in town," I remark.

I have no idea what's about to happen and I need a break. I'm not used to all this talking. I'm turning the next section over to our Narrator. He's got an eye for detail. He can set the stage.

So what if he likes Noir the most? It hasn't messed up the story has it?

A WHOLE LOT OF PATIENCE INVOLVED

A handwritten signboard is posted on a residential lawn as Noir drives into Cedar Harbor.

How'd Mayor Karvonen Buy His New Truck?

"Dollars to donuts the convent signs and this one are related," Kirkallen asserts. "Methinks we're witnessing small town politics up close and personal." He rubs his hands together. A conspiratorial gesture.

The village is laid out in a neat compact grid. Avenues bear typical or regionally branded names.

Superior.

Front.

Main.

Lake.

Cedar.

Commerce.

Minnesota.

Any moderately ambulatory soul can take in the sights with a leisurely twenty-minute stroll. He can discover businesses lacking chain store affiliation that provide the stuff to keep a town functional.

An IGA, a pharmacy, a tavern, a Louis Sullivan bank, a pizzeria, post office, medical clinic, large animal vet and an unassuming Lutheran church with an outsized spire. There's Amundsen's Hardware, Fuel, Hunting & Fishing Emporium. The Blue Plate Diner advertises its daily special menu. Big Lake Coffee & Beans markets a shade-grown product. Lake Country Realty sells vacation and retirement dreams. The American Legion produces weekend suppers. Superior Brewing evidently opened recently, obvious by its fresh scrubbed appearance. The trio passes the Cedar County Sheriff Substation, Canoe Country Outfitters, Kristiansen's Small Engine Repair, Harbor Side B&B and WCED Radio. A smattering of artists and tradesmen have set up shop, eager to gain commercial footholds.

The town continues to work as an integral unit, a rarity for a small community. Isolation is at once an impediment as well as a factor contributing to economic vibrancy.

At first glimpse Cedar Harbor feels friendly and comfortable. A place where you'd like to hang and drink a beer. But the signs taped to the insides of store windows and punched into front lawns are ominous, more than hinting at discord.

Save The Convent.

DSG Go Home.

"Whoa," Noir says as they reach the village outskirts, "talk about Negative Waves back there?"

Without hesitation she delivers an edited version of a classic Bogart quote from *To Have and Have Not.* "We may have landed right in the middle of a small war."

"Turn left. Here," Hardy prompts. "Up the hill is where we're going. I think. To the House on the Hill."

The ridge ascent is steep and winding. It's lined with slender birch and gray scaly-barked jack pine.

Kirkallen assesses the drive. "I'd hate to shovel this." He holds the same winter obligation at his Saint Paul abode. That's the chore he ceded to Hardy when his back gave out.

The home is impressive. The sprawling three-floor mansion, seemingly a pair of separate and identically designed structures, is inventively stitched together by a builder who likely covered his mistakes with cedar shingles and by diverting critical eyes from design flaws with stained glass, elegantly carved porch columns, corner towers and hidden balconies.

There's a rickety well house and, judging by the feathered animals pecking the nearby grounds, an active chicken coop. A small barn, a paddock behind it, stands sturdy and used. It sits beside a carriage house with second floor dormers. An apartment for the hired help. A red-and-white-striped open-walled tent beckons expectantly in the side yard. At the edge of the forest a cluster of guest cottages, doors invitingly flung open, yearns for occupants.

The eclectic building assemblage, the flower, herb and vegetable gardens, hint at self-sufficiency as if formerly occupied by an extended family unit.

Cars are parked at odd angles along the edges of the circular drive. The grassy center island is staked with *Save The Convent* signs. Black letters on a white background.

Noir finds space among the vehicles and eases the Forester to a halt. She switches off the engine and stretches. Muskie rises beside her and mimics her mistress. The group focuses on drink-holding wedding guests mingling on the spacious wraparound veranda, its floor painted a deep blue, white railings laced with festive tricolored bunting. A collection of scarlet Adirondack chairs lines the wall. Baskets of pansies hang, at intervals, from the porch lintel. They sway with the breeze over a flowering hedge.

Hardy's nervous anticipatory sigh interrupts the pregnant silence inside the car, which not even Kirkallen can break.

"Well. We've arrived. I expect I'm as ready as I'm ever gonna be to stare fate in the eye. Besides meeting my estranged daughter, it will be interesting to meet my son-in-law-to-be. And yeah there's Abby. What sounded like a good idea an hour ago now sounds like a harebrained scheme."

"Don't force it my brother," Kirkallen counsels. "Let it come to you. In due time. It's the Navajo Way."

"Your Navajo must like trout fishing," Hardy remarks sourly.

Kirkallen has a knack for interpreting his friend's non sequitur-ish comments. "Precisely. There's a whole lot of patience involved."

Only Muskie senses something unusual, an Out of the Ordinary Presence. She emits a low and expectant whine. She twitches her tail ever so slightly.

Let's continue to wonder what she's onto. If anything.

As Narrator, the storyteller, I hope I've helped you picture the place. I think it will get more interesting if we check out what others are thinking and feeling and saying. I'll let them tell you.

LONG-LOST DAUGHTER

A tall and robust woman steps hesitantly off the porch. Gently. As if she suspects the ground will buckle. Maybe it will.

I can't believe this is happening.

She approaches. Cautiously. She's wearing her mom's blonde hair, this version cut to shoulder length and parted neatly. It glistens in the sun. She's taller than Heather but Heather was a better athlete. Libby didn't care for the competition. She's sturdier too. She carries her bulk comfortably. It fits without excess on her jean-clad frame.

This is my long-lost daughter.

The Girl Who Left.

The Girl I Kicked Out of Our House.

Libby, our Afterthought Child.

I don't know what to do or how to act.

Do I hug her? Is there a Style Manual to tell you what to do when reuniting with an estranged child? Please forward it to me.

What I know thus far is what I see.

She looks good. Happy. Her face glows. Her eyes shine clear and bright. She is in love.

I can't believe it. She's smiling. At me.

I am also tongue-tied. "Libby" is all I can stutter.

"Father," she says deliberately.

This is awkward. She's never called me *Father*. It's always been *Dad*.

"I'm Elizabeth now." Her correction is genial but firm.

"All right. I didn't know. That's fair ... Elizabeth. Daughter. I'm pleased to see you. It's been too long. That's my fault. All of it."

"Well there is that," she allows as she gives me an ocular once-over.

The next part is delivered like she's prepared it. She's glad to see me. She hopes we can let bygones be gone. How good it would be, she says, if we could get along over the next few days. This is a very special occasion. A Life Event she wants to share with her family. All Her Family.

I guess *All* includes me.

Translation? She may not truly be happy to see me. Her steady and open gaze is tinged with traces of uncertainty. Time will tell. As it stands she's making it clear she's prepared to put up with me.

Basically I've been told politely: *Don't screw this up.*

I won't.

I tell her I bet these are hard words for her to say and I thank her for saying them. I say I hope we can be easy with each other and maybe even find space in our hearts for forgiveness.

This is nothing I prepared. In fact I tried hard not to think about what I might say. I figured I'd let the Muse Who Spoke for Me in the Gayle Harte Meeting go for it.

It feels like it's working. Stuff is simply spewing out of my mouth. It's genuine. It's coming from my heart. That can't be all bad.

This New Me? Uttering legit feelings? Whoa.

I'm admitting I do miss my daughter. You also heard me Own Up by accepting blame and fault for our schism. Both spoken acknowledgements surprise me. My Old Self could be a tad—actually more than a tad—stubborn.

There you have it. The truth.

You know that Pride Thing? The Pride Thing fueled by testosterone? I'm trying to let it go.

This is what I said.

"I'm sorry for being an asshole. That New Year's Eve? I could have eased off. Should have eased off. I hope you can find it in your heart to forgive me. And please forgive my continued unforgiving behavior. There's no place for that in our brief life spans. I shouldn't have treated you like I did."

I've caught her off guard with my honesty. I don't think she understands I'm amazing myself too. I extend my hand and we shake.

We're not quite up to hugging.

I hope that comes in due time.

Then her truth comes out.

"I promised myself I'd welcome you," she says seriously. "Believe it or not there are people in our family who insisted on inviting you. But if you mean what you're saying I'm glad we did. You've taken a big stride toward trying to make things right. I appreciate the Olive Branch. You needed to offer it. So for the time being meet my Alex."

She keeps her eyes fixed on mine and calls over her shoulder. "Alex, honey? Come here, please? Meet my father. The guy I've told you about."

Alex approaches, speaking deliberately with a pleasant drawl, "Elizabeth's stories about y'all haven't been altogether charitable. But some good's been thrown in with the bad. I like to think I'm mature enough to make up my own mind. Welcome to The House on the Hill. I own this place. It's my home ... I should say *We own this place. It's our home.* And you're our welcome guest. We're delighted you've joined us."

So I meet Alex, who's convivially Southern and looks me in the eye and offers a firm handshake and truly appears to like Libby. But I'm blown away since the first thing I notice about Alex is she's not a guy.

"I'm Alexandra Kerr. I prefer *Alexandra* to *Alex* but Elizabeth does like using my more familiar name. I don't mind."

She is petite and dignified and requires no makeup to highlight her plain and simple beauty. Her deep red hair, rich with curl and body, is pulled into a tight bun, revealing an honest face and green eyes.

I should break in here and tell you I'm not opposed to gay marriage or anything like that. I figure there's room in this world for all different kinds of healthy relationships. Besides I have no interest in discovering what couples do in the privacy of their own bedrooms as long as they treat each other with respect. If Elizabeth has found a good friend to walk through life with all the better for her. I'm fine with it.

Privately? Remember how in Doc's office I told you I had that Extra Radar Screen? I think I knew Libby was gay before she did. That guy with his hands all over her? I think it was her desperate attempt to say *See I'm trying to be straight and this is my awkward way of showing it to you. That's one reason why this is such an awkward moment.* I can't tell you why I sensed this about Libby but I did.

While I attempt to come to terms with this Unexpected Manifestation and try to process these thoughts as rapidly as possible the Girl in Black strides right up to the Happy Couple as if she's tossing me a verbal life buoy. She acts like she knows them or has at least met them. That also feels odd but I don't press. I've got enough to process.

Noir grabs Kirkallen's hand. She identifies him as a Good Guy. She tells the girls how she loves us. We've given her a home and while folks think it's weird she lives with us, it's the best place she's ever lived. She finishes the thought by paraphrasing Gladys George from *The Roaring Twenties*.

"They're decent guys. And decent guys are hard to find."

Noir barely takes a breath. She shifts gears. She continues with how delighted she is to be included in the wedding festivities to which Elizabeth says *We wouldn't have it otherwise.*

I'm witnessing a straight up Love Fest and a side of Noir I've not seen. She's speaking in longer sentences. Even sharing some feelings. I've certainly never heard her say anything about loving us.

Nice to hear.

No wonder she's good at her admissions work. The girl can be downright personable.

All of a sudden the women are hugging and I'm getting the idea Noir might be lesbian too.

She does own a Subaru.

I've never asked her about her love life and she's never offered.

One thing for sure? I ain't asking. She can tell me if she wants.

And Kirkallen? Maybe Kirkallen already knows. The man loves to talk but I know he can keep his peace.

Next thing I know Kirkallen dismisses the query about his white garter with *This is not a time for politics* and goes all Hillerman on the smiling group, talking the Beauty Way and *hozro*. He concludes with a compliment for The House on the Hill about how the *Dineh* would like that the front door faces east. To the rising sun.

Never mind a traditional Hogan has one door. He omitted that.

Afterwards kind of all blends together into a set of remembered visions.

Kirkallen and Noir and I mount the porch and meet folks and sip iced teas and snack on Vermont cheddar and crackers and smoked lake trout.

Muskie prances up on the veranda with us. She immediately stretches contentedly on the cushion of half of a vacant double occupancy wooden glider, her tail thumping slightly while the chair keeps time with her. Or she with it.

Must be something going on. She doesn't even graze for dropped or abandoned snacks.

Finally an older African-American woman approaches and introduces herself as Marion. She says she lives at The Convent but manages the estate for the girls. "They mean well but they do stumble over each other. I keep them on point. I let them think they run The House and that they're running their own wedding. But I am. I want to make sure you feel welcome so may I show you to your quarters?"

As we chat with Marion and angle toward the guest cottages, Muskie reluctantly follows. She trails resolutely behind Noir but casts backward glances toward the porch.

With the approaching solstice and forty-seven degrees of latitude it'll be light 'til well into the evening. We're invited to a late supper at a cookout in town. By the harbor. There's a political gig going on. The organizers are down there now doing setup. It's something about saving The Convent. Yeah the one referenced in the signs we've read.

We're gonna eat grilled sausages and beans and potato salad and listen to live music. There'll be speeches too.

I have zero interest in The Politics of Cedar Harbor. I'm only happy to have left my Former Life in Local Politics in the rear view mirror.

But the promise of an open keg—a popular Superior Brewing pale ale, Portage Rest—is intriguing. Elizabeth says the brewery owner will be there. She says he's a good man. She says he takes his craft beer seriously. So they tease him by calling him *Milwaukee*.

I'm looking forward to the picnic. It should be fun. But I'm feeling stressed after meeting Elizabeth and Alexandra. I'm returning this tale to our Narrator. I think he might want to make a confession.

LIBERAL BUT EVEN MINDED THINKERS

Hardy's thrown the narrative to me because he needs a break. He's also figured out I have an admission to make.

I'm trying to be a dispassionate nonpartisan observer. I'm trying to illuminate the facts and let you make the assumptions. However, listening to Hardy and Noir is drawing me into the narrative in a more personal way than anticipated.

And Noir's right. I do like her the best. She's caught my eye. That's why I introduced her to the other female characters and brought her to The House on the Hill. I want to keep her involved. I do understand I have to be careful not to play favorites but you should be aware of my predilection and check me if I get carried away.

I've also heard Hardy say I can't turn the story over to Kirkallen. He said I'll never get it back if I do. I can't afford that. I'm losing control of the narrative as it is.

I do have authority to speak here. I know about Alexandra Kerr and I'm going to tell you about her. Since I'm inventing this stuff it's all you're ever going to know.

Alexandra owns The House on the Hill, an estate unexpectedly passed down via a distant familial relationship dating to seventeenth century Ireland. Something vague about her Scot-Irish relatives' emigration to America because, as Presbyterians, they couldn't own the land they farmed in northeast Ireland. Land Queen Elizabeth I usurped from rightful Irish Catholic owners when she began *Plantationizing* Ulster. The bloodline moves through seven generations to a Minnesota lumber baron's renegade son who moved to Charlotte in the early twentieth century and operated a successful business there.

Alexandra's parents hoped for a boy. They planned to name him *Alexander* after a particularly singular distant cousin, Alexander Craighead, a Donegal-born kid who traveled with his father to America on the same boat with Alexandra's more direct relatives. They arrived in New England in the early 1700s.

Ordained to the Presbyterian ministry in the 1730s, Craighead's liberal attitudes, peppery tongue and anti-royalist public tirades earned him banishment from two Presbyteries. He finally found a home in a frontier settlement where he set up shop at the intersection of two trade routes located on the edge of Tuscarora country in the western Carolinas. Craighead founded seven colonial churches, helped *Civilize* the area and earned the reputation as a community leader.

I won't delve any deeper into why I italicized *Civilize*. You know why. It's the same reason I italicized *Plantationizing*. We don't have the space to address the issue of the subjugation of peoples in detail and I don't want to get bogged down in political debate. I don't want to mess up this story by bringing the Real World into it. Let's keep to the topic at hand.

Two centuries later, when the baby they hoped to name for Craighead emerged from her mother's womb with a different sexual apparatus than anticipated, the well-to-do and socially connected parents named their girl-child *Alexandra*.

She attended posh Southern boarding schools where she learned good manners and to think critically and analytically. She proved as opinionated and stubborn as her Craighead namesake. She needed three years to graduate *Cum Laude* from Vanderbilt. Then, to extreme parental dismay, she ventured out on her own.

She traveled solo in Europe, found nanny work in France and returned home when her parents died unexpectedly, tragically, in a single car accident. Shortly after their funeral she discovered she'd inherited a bank load of cash and investments as well as a rundown mansion in northeast Minnesota. Accordingly she set out for the Cold North Country, intent on finding her life's direction, unwittingly reversing the career path of her distant cousin, the lumber baron's son.

When she found the estate in disrepair, maintained by an off-site overseer who did nothing more than keep the place dry and sound, she assumed residence and pitched in. She began with the headstones overlooking an expansive stretch of Lake Superior.

The graves of relatives she never knew, and never knew she had, reposed in an overgrown cedar grove.

Robert and Margaret Kerr.

Leah and Rachel Kerr.

Cousins several times removed.

Alexandra rooted out the brush and weeds. She restored the stones and laid down a cedar chip path that connected the site with the mansion's rear door. She constructed an Aldo Leopold-style bench out of rough cut lumber and set it by the grave plot. The site evolved into her sanctuary. She continues to greet the morning there in that seat as she savors a cup of tea while surveying the inscrutable lake.

It took time and effort and money but Alexandra had all three. Locals gradually opened their hearts to the polite and charmingly Southern girl. A couple years into her bold restoration project, a good friend referred a pair of elderly women to her. Women who'd traveled north to attend a retreat at the nearby convent and wanted to stay on.

They readily agreed to help with house rehab in exchange for a roof over their heads and a willingness to contribute to the communal pantry. The women exhibited a grand touch with vegetable and herb and garden plots. They planted asparagus rows, raspberry patches, flowering bulbs, hardy fruit trees, a grape arbor, a butterfly garden. They tapped maples when the sap ran.

Everything worked perfectly.

The women found a home and connected to the town. They volunteered at The Convent, sold vegetables at the farmers market they started and expressed interest in community politics. They hosted their own WCED radio show and earned reputations as outspoken liberal but even minded thinkers who listened carefully and respectfully to all sides of any dispute.

Not so gradually the women strengthened their emotional bond with Alexandra, a young woman they began treating like a daughter. All the more reason for the gray haired ladies to stay. In time they introduced Alexandra to their daughters.

Then the David Shire Group bought The Convent of the Holy Sisters. That spelled trouble. We'll find out more about that next. At the picnic.

HE KNOWS THEM BOTH

Micah Hardy is flummoxed by his recent reunion, superficial as it might be, with Elizabeth. And with discovering she's a lesbian. You know he's not upset by her revelation. But he is surprised. It's a bulky idea he's trying to wrap his brain around. Primarily because he understands his daughter's life may be more difficult than it needs to be.

He also feels relieved.

Elizabeth talked to him. She seemed to welcome him. As did Alexandra. A good place to start.

He's standing with Kirkallen on the harbor beach sipping a draft pale ale. Kirkallen holds a Kaliber, one of two non-alcoholic beverages Noir brought for him. Later on, at The House, he and Hardy will pass a pipe. Then the world will glisten and life's harder edges will soften.

The Lads are sipping their drinks. They're wearing Celtic sweaters over fishing shirts. The air tastes sweet and cool, freshly scrubbed. They watch Noir and Muskie mingle. Noir's dressed less severely noir so the more straightlaced won't get nervous. Her harem pants and flowing long sleeve blouse balloon in the light breeze. Muskie trails in Noir's wake. She's content to munch on abandoned plates of sausages and beans. Her mustache, the one Hardy trims, sports a greasy shine.

A flotilla of recently launched sail boats—sloops, ketches and yawls—bobs in the harbor, tugging gently at their moorings. Working boats, herring seiners, are tethered to a nearby dock. A common merganser, the rear of its rusty head needing combing, paddles in the protected water. She totes three newly hatched chicks on her back.

"All that's missing is the salt smell," Kirkallen muses.

"Huh?"

"Superior doesn't smell of salt. I miss the ocean," he admits. "But not enough to want to move there."

"Ladies and Gentlemen. Citizens of all stripes," a voice calls through a PA system. "Attention please."

The speaker is a wiry elderly female. One of the Sisters. She raises her arms to settle the crowd and introduces the primary spokespersons. She motions toward two women who will give a joint presentation.

Hardy jerks involuntarily, as if poked by a cattle prod.

He knows them both.

I can't read his mind but Hardy looks like he's ready to be Somewhere Else. Immediately. Maybe taking that toke up at The House. Let's tune in to what's happening.

I'M EIGHTEEN AND DUMB

I recognize her in an instant. I haven't seen her, barely thought of her, in over forty years. And there she is standing on the podium. Standing next to my wife and readying to give a political speech in Cedar Harbor, Minnesota.

How to tell you about Hannah?

Let's do like our Narrator suggests in his third chapter reference to *The Wizard of Oz.*

"It's always best to start at the beginning."

I'm a Long Island boy and I played high school hoops. We had decent teams and won our county championship two years running. I

of the earth country folk. They don't know what to make of their feisty daughter. Especially when she says *Southwest's full ride scholarship offer is too good to pass up.*

What did she mean?

I'm in love with my high school sweetheart and Kansas is too far from home.

Samuel lives nearby. Hannah thinks her guy is The One.

Like me, Hannah is a Fish out of Water at Southwest State. She marches to a different cadence than her Standard Brand Lutheran Schoolmates.

They puzzle her.

I admire her from afar. Off and on in the library or cafeteria. Occasionally across the room at a party.

I learn what dorm she lives in. Comstock. When I pass her building I always look for her.

We are finally introduced in the spring of our sophomore year and hit it off. Obviously I think Hannah's beautiful.

She is.

She's five-six-ish and slightly built with narrow hips and small breasts. Muscled like a farm girl. Forearms like iron.

Her hair's a rich dark brown and naturally thick with body. All I can think is I want to run my fingers through it.

For hours.

Her face is ruddy with sun. She sees the world through wide set brown eyes. Her smile knocks me over.

We spend a lot of time together and get to kissing but nothing heavy.

Hannah is honest about it. She says she loves Samuel.

I'm an Exotic Temptation.

A non-Mennonite from the East Coast.

I'm so blinded by Hannah I don't care if I'm treated like a Sociological Experiment. I figure given time she can love me.

Instead.

It's Finals Week before I know it. Summer break arrives far too soon. We go home.

During the spring of that year I studied Shakespeare and wished for the best with Hannah. Like the sonnet I hoped "summer's lease" would have "way too short a date."

Summer's not short enough to keep Hannah and Samuel apart.

When we return to school she immediately and determinedly backs off. We're too different. We're not a good match. She loves Samuel. She delivers that famous line no guy likes to hear.

I like you as a friend.

It's a dagger to my heart.

Deep down I know she's lying. To herself. I feel it.

There's nothing I can do about it.

I know what I can't do though.

I can't be Hannah's friend. It hurts too much.

I date a girl I don't really like. She ends it after we drink a few and start necking and I call her *Hannah.*

The academic year continues its inexorable pace. I try not to see her. I learn her class and dining schedules and studiously avoid her. When our paths cross we avoid eye contact. No words exchanged.

Though it kills me when I see her, I learn to search the gym for her during home games. She sits in the top row, up in a corner by herself, behind the visitors' bench.

After hoops season ends, and entirely out of the blue, Hannah gets drunk for the first time and comes for me. She's hugging a mostly emptied bottle of Boone's Farm like a long-lost friend.

Jesus what a vision.

Her brown eyes glow. Her lips shine and her hair's slipping out of the bun she tied it in. There's an additional button loose on her blouse and yeah I look.

I look but I don't know what to do. I'm in a jam.

She's drunk and coming on. She drapes her arms around my neck and whispers things in my ear that aren't the Hannah I know. Plus she's wearing perfume. Canoe? I know that's not Her either.

On the other hand she is saying she wants what I want and I know I want my hands all over her.

But deep down I know this: I know What I Want and What's Right are different things.

I tell her she's drunk and we should cool it and we do. I escort her to her dorm, more or less carrying her as we go. She thanks me at the door and we say goodnight and I think that's it.

I regret my Honorable Decision on the walk home. Likely my one and only chance.

The chance I know I wanted. But I wanted it on even terms.

No regrets on either side.

She finds me in the library the next day and apologizes and thanks me again and we start hanging out and get to kissing more and more and summer comes and we go home and write extended, heartfelt of letters to each other 'cause it's too expensive to call long distance and besides the phones in our respective houses are located in the kitchens and make privacy hard to come by.

Hannah breaks up with Samuel that summer.

We spend senior year in lockstep, never too far removed from each other's sight. We study together, take classes together, eat together, dance together, do laundry together and play together.

The thing we don't do together is the thing I want most.

We sleep in our own dormitory beds.

It's not like I'm not trying. I want into her pants real bad but she's too much the Good Mennonite Girl for that. She carries her creed close to her heart. She keeps her blue jeans on.

Understand this is the spring of 1970. Even the Kent State shootings are receiving moderate air play in conservative southwest Minnesota. We read about Woodstock and the Summer of Love, watched Martin and Bobby get shot and listened to news broadcasts about the Chicago Convention riots. We heard Tricky Dick lie to us. We couldn't understand why so many U.S. troops were dying in Southeast Asia. And what for?

It is a tumultuous time to be young. Dylan's right. The times are changing.

Our generation's so naïve we think we're the first ever to understand that fact.

So kids my age are asking hard questions. Flaunting authority. Acting spacy and liberated. Smoking weed. Discarding underwear and growing their hair long.

Regardless, Hannah Penner is Hannah Penner. Going All the Way has to wait 'til marriage.

What I'm saying is all my buddies are getting laid, or they're saying they are, and I'm not.

I love Hannah Penner. I'm willing to wait.

Things go haywire late in that semester when the serious interest I express in the church as a tool for social change and in the lifestyles of Christian activists, William Stringfellow and Daniel Berrigan, prompts a belated acceptance to a New Jersey seminary.

I talk about being a minister.

Hannah's Mennonite. She isn't sure about moving to Princeton with me, compromising her cultural roots. The word she uses is *betraying*. She can't see herself as a Presbyterian minister's wife.

Do you blame her?

As hard as we try to love each other the future is arriving and running us down. It isn't pretty.

On graduation eve we introduce our families and share a down-home chicken and dumpling supper at a family style restaurant. After we bid good night and Hannah escorts her folks to the hotel, she comes and knocks on my door and I'm inside drinking suds with my buds. She pulls me out into the hall and kisses me warmly.

She's not going home.

It's our first time but it is a sweet evening. No need to go into detail other than we're clumsy and awkward.

As we lie there afterward the thunder booms for real. A torrential Minnesota storm. Lightning flashes and illuminates her body.

I think I've died and gone to heaven. Either that or I'm privy to an exclusive viewing in the Louvre.

If I peer carefully into my memory I clearly see that picture.

We graduate under a huge striped tent set up on the quad. We smile and pose for pictures as Hannah's heels sink into the rain softened turf.

It's over and done.

I drive home with my folks to prepare for grad school. Hannah stops writing and refuses to return my calls, let alone take them. Isaac tells me politely but firmly not to call. He says Hannah's gone to work with the Mennonite Disaster Service. He calls me a *nice boy* but says I'm Presbyterian and she's Mennonite. If I loved and respected her I'd also respect his daughter's wishes and stop trying to reach her.

I'm twenty-one and broke.

If Hannah's parents aren't telling the truth and she is home I'm thirteen hundred miles away from her. If she's not there I don't even know where to begin looking. I don't own a car. I don't have enough cash to travel. I've enrolled in summer school at the seminary. Biblical Greek is demanding all of my attention. Twelve hours a day for an accelerated class. Fifteen semester weeks crammed into four.

All I keep from the ghost of that relationship is a graduation photograph. Me and Hannah arm in arm, gowns open to reveal her modest high necked dress and my blazer and tie. We were never Flower Children.

The next time I see Hannah is over forty years later at a picnic in Cedar Harbor, Minnesota. She's standing next to my wife, Abigael Delaney.

This wedding is getting curiouser and curiouser.

A FIGURATIVE SMACK UPSIDE HARDY'S HEAD

The sight of Abby Delaney and Hannah Penner on stage delivers a figurative smack upside Hardy's head.

Takes his breath away.

Puts a pit in his gut.

Buckles his knees.

"Jesus!" he gasps and repeats the name.

He's speaking aloud. Really loud. He doesn't realize it.

Heads pivot in the gathered throng. Among an eclectic collection of lumberjack types, their faces tanned by a combination of spring sunshine and snow glare, there are homemakers, business people, truck drivers, artists, artisans, fishing and hunting guides—a group salted generously by gray headed retirees.

One female gray head frowns disapprovingly at him. "Shhh."

It's a harsh sound and more heads turn and stare.

Hardy mouths an inaudible *Sorry*. He wants passionately to disappear. Tough to do when you're six-seven.

The speakers are occupied with their agenda and do not notice him. Hardy eases out of the crowd while whispering urgently to his friends and gesturing frantically to them.

Kirkallen and Noir and Hardy convene discreetly on the rocky shingle behind a thick growth of alder. Noir begins, "You understood Abby would be doing her political thing? What gives?"

"I didn't think she'd be speaking," Hardy responds. "All Heather tells me about her mom is she's gotten involved in social causes. It's all I need to know. All I want to know."

"Until now, evidently," Kirkallen deadpans.

"It would've helped if I'd known," Hardy admits. "I could've been more prepared if you guys clued me in about her being on stage but that's a minor point. I can deal with it."

"What else?" Noir queries.

"You know the other lady up there?" he nods at the podium. "Ever seen her?"

"Yeah. That's Hannah. Abby's good buddy. I've met her once or twice. She's a nice lady. So?"

"I've met her once or twice myself."

"Huh."

"Last time I saw her she was my serious college girlfriend. Like real serious. She broke it off and I never knew why. She went home after graduation and stopped talking to me. I tried to reach her but her grandpa did the talking for her. He said if I loved and respected her I'd leave her alone. I couldn't reach her. She never reached out to me. That's all I know."

"Far out," says Kirkallen.

He's chuckling.

The trio holds on to the silence, digesting Hardy's intelligence and their circumstances.

Kirkallen breaks their reverie.

"Out of sight. This is too rich. You know the *Dineh* believe you can't hold on to a bitter past, right?" He lightly punches Hardy's shoulder. "It's time to let it all go. You can't see it, my man, but this is an outstanding opportunity to tie up a bunch of loose ends in your life. They're right in front of you right now. Your long-lost daughter. Her lesbian partner. Your estranged wife. And surprise, a former serious girlfriend? One you haven't seen or heard from in forty years? Out of sight, man. Out of effing sight."

Noir grins and gives Hardy an oblique hug. She has a Robert Montgomery line ready. "Some cases like this one kind of creep up on you on their hands and knees. The next thing you know you're in it up to your neck."

Kirkallen arches his eyebrows at her.

"*Lady in the Lake*. 1947, I think." Then she smiles. Angelic. "Kirky, we're in for some serious fun this weekend, aren't we?"

Kirky. Noir's the only one he lets call him that. He despises his given name. Harwood.

Kirkallen replies, "You dig we offered two takes on the same set of circumstances? Navajo and Film Noir? But we've come to the same conclusion."

He pivots as the crowd comes to life with a murmur of applause. "Let's check out what the ladies have to say. I wonder if we can throw more ingredients into our cauldron."

Noir cites the seventeenth century Bard. "'Double, double, toil and trouble ...'"

"Fire burns and my butt bubbles," Hardy allows.

"Get your *hozro* on," Kirkallen encourages. "Walk in Beauty."

Noir simplifies. "It's time to buckle up your Big Boy Pants, Pops."

The women are finishing when the trio rejoins the assemblage and Hardy considers the pair. Seasoned women clad in jeans and flannel button-downs, their faces etched finely with age and a knowing confidence in their maturity.

The Feisty Elder Female Types who loved to give him a pain in the ass at community public hearings. In spite of his tension he breathes a sigh of relief. He hasn't once missed his job.

Abby Delaney is winding up her rant, "On top of the construction, DSG plans to build a golf course. We all know people play many stupid games in this world but don't you think golf ruins the most acreage and wastes the most water?"

She waits for a smattering of applause to abate. "You'll come out with us? On Monday?" she implores. "Seven in the morning? Fight the eviction? Meet at the entrance to The Convent drive. We need you there. I promise you'll see more than you expect. The bottom line is we must stop the heavy equipment from entering our property. No way DSG razes The Convent of the Holy Sisters."

Hardy can't help but feel a moment of pride as he realizes how much his wife has grown. How strong she is. How confidently she carries herself. *I was all she needed until she didn't.*

Hannah Penner adds closing thoughts. "We do need you to come out, friends. Solidarity is vital. But remember, come with peaceful intentions." She clenches her fist and raises it above her head. As defiant and proud as Tommie Smith raising his fisted black glove on the medal stand at the 1968 Olympics.

Abby concludes. "Thanks for coming. Thanks for listening. Thanks for being our friends. Let's go empty that keg and finish off the grub."

"Amen," Hannah affirms.

Hardy shrugs. "So be it."

THEY PROVE A STURDY FLOCK

The Convent is not a convent in the proper sense of Roman Catholic religious orders. At the turn of the twentieth century a company of forward-thinking nuns—outcasts or voluntary exiles from contemplative, teaching and monastic traditions—seek a place to call their own. Intent on serving, praying, worshipping and living in community in their own distinctive fashion, the original posse flees north, eschewing the hustle and bustle of a changing America. They coax a lumber baron into building them a home and chapel on the edge of a growing Lake Superior hamlet.

Robert Kerr agrees to their terms. As long as they participate actively in community life and provide a place of worship for his Catholic laborers.

"I don't care if you're priests or not," Kerr declares. "My men and their families need Communion on Sundays."

The *Sisters*, as the town folk call them, and as they call one another, wear traditional habits and circulate in and about the village as necessity and interest dictate. They teach school, take in laundry, do clerical work, staff the library and provide aid to the less fortunate. To their absolute delight they preside over daily Mass and one on the Sabbath day.

They prove a sturdy flock. They milk their own cows, churn butter, produce cheese, butcher and process their fowl, livestock, hogs and game. They can and freely distribute their surplus garden bounty. Robert quietly arranges for various deliveries of Lake Superior's wealth. As well as gratefully accepted sides of venison. In and out of season.

The Sisters gradually discard their habits in favor of more practical dress. The Old Sisters die and the Young Sisters stop arriving. The Remaining Sisters open their doors to women, and women's groups, of all monotheistic stripes. Even a few stray Buddhists. These visitors seek, or need, spiritual renewal. Strengthening and enlightenment. Others simply desire contemplative retreats.

The shrewd move keeps The Convent afloat. Barely.

Several years ago an independent and ecumenical group of freethinking women fronts the cash to buy the place. The New Sisters move in with the Remaining Ones. They spruce up the landscape, open their grounds and gardens to the community and focus their attention on their new home. They form a corporation.

While engaging local contractors and labor to supplement their willing work force, the Sisters paint, carpenter, plumb and improve the physical plant. They even dig a new well. The upgrade contributes positively to the economy by attracting tourist trade to Cedar Harbor.

More importantly their efforts earn favor with the Town Council and the general citizenry.

As needs arise Cedar County Bank works with them when they require cash for infrastructure repairs. But ultimately a project emerges requiring deeper pockets and the Sisters err by approaching a Twin Cities bank, which generates an unfortunate business interest. An investment coalition, the David Shire Group, takes a shine to the place. DSG sees dollar signs.

Then Mayor Karvonen enters the fray. Considered a relative newcomer by locals he'd moved up from the Cities about a decade before. They'd called him on his name's Finnish derivation when he arrived and claimed Swedish heritage. They should know. As late as 1910 almost ninety percent of the population north of Duluth owned foreign-born heritage. Most of them were Finns.

In spite of his cultural ignorance, Karvonen proved inoffensive enough as he forged political inroads and gained modest approval. Eventually he ran unopposed for mayor and took office.

When DSG arrives, the perceived power goes to Karvonen's head. He gets greedy. He enthusiastically boards the Development Bandwagon.

It doesn't take long for the city fathers to see dollar signs too.

They claim a condo complex will bring new cash, new blood, new interests to town. Including the insertion of a nine hole golf course into The Convent hillside.

DSG, the Town Council and Karvonen question the legality of the Holy Sisters' incorporation. And zoning? They discover, or invent, property and food service code violations.

Some residents start asking questions.

Why is the mayor driving a new Chevy pickup? Especially when sleazebag David Shire owns at least four car dealerships?

Bottom line? Cedar Harbor's Town Council unearths sufficient violations to condemn The Convent and assumes Eminent Domain.

The mayor doesn't have the Gorgonzolas to post the eviction notice on the Sisters' front door. He makes his secretary do it.

❖

A NEGATIVE VOCAL AND UNCOUNTED BALLOT

Abigael Delaney and Hannah Penner meet while pursuing personal retreats at The Convent of the Holy Sisters. They each take a room there to spend a week in quiet and private reflection.

They become acquainted over meals and at prayer services. Each takes interest in the other's Faith Journey.

Abby the devout and literal Roman Catholic.

Hannah a progressive Mennonite.

Regardless of their theosophical differences the attraction is instant and mutual. A friendship blossoms. When they return to their Twin Cities homes one thing leads to two more.

They begin conducting interfaith workshops. They incorporate. They gain notoriety as the popularity of their program goes regional and they travel to conduct retreats. They train workshop leaders to meet growing demand. The media takes note.

They hire a secretary. He develops a website and a marketing plan. He solicits donors and develops a scholarship program. They go national. To Berkeley, Seattle, Tucson, Richmond and Atlanta. Even Salt Lake City. Then on to Dublin and Rouen and Amsterdam.

They're making money but they've lost their spiritual focus and they know it. The business is easy to sell to a group of eager younger women.

In need of spiritual refreshment and battery recharging Abby and Hannah retreat once again to Cedar Harbor. That's how they got here.

A willingness to provide a cash infusion for The Convent gives them seats at the board of directors' table.

A friendship with House on the Hill owner, Alexandra Kerr, puts a roof over their heads.

In short order they're taxpaying residents. Walking sections of the Superior Hiking Trail, canoeing nearby lakes, producing their own maple syrup, working the gardens at The House. They mix in town politics and become popular radio show hosts.

They make one huge mistake. They approach a Twin Cities bank for help with an infrastructure project at The Convent. The David Shire Group arrives.

Earlier this year when the Town Council voted to condemn The Convent of the Holy Sisters, employing a variety of spurious rationales, only one person registered a negative vocal and uncounted ballot. Its singular female member. The one whose interest in the property required her to recuse herself from the process.

The singular female? Abigael Delaney.

"Those bastards couldn't buy me," she said.

Strong words from a staunch Christian who swears off swearing.

SO THIS IS MY LIFE

I told you about Hannah and me to tell you the truth. Not to engage your sympathy. It's a sad story if you think it is. It's what happened. I gradually forgot about her. Time healed my wounds. There's not even a scar. At least not one I can see.

I hope Hannah's not scarred. Since she ended it I never thought about that. Until now.

Thinking back on that time? I find it ironic that my interest in the ministry is what chased Hannah away.

You know I never became a minister. Given my religious confusions, you know that's for the very best. I'd've made a shitty one anyway.

What I do regret about not choosing the ministry is I never found a professional direction. Then I went completely off the rails when I became The Political Heavy for the College of St. Rose.

I accept the fact I played The Ruthless Assassin. I accepted the job. I accepted the paycheck. I have to live with that.

I'll spend the rest of my time making up for it.

Thank God Gayle Harte saved me by giving me The Hook. I'd like to believe I would have left anyway.

You know I was about to.

Harte made it easier. I didn't have to take The Risk. She made it easy by paying me to leave.

Bottom line? I'm not worried about whether I would've quit my job or not.

I'm not working.

And I have the time to pay attention to what matters.

My relationships. My family. My life.

I met Abby a couple of years after Hannah and I split. We loved each other. For a while. In some weird way we probably still do.

I tried to be open and honest with her. You know it backfired. Think about it. My wanting to be a minister screwed up one relationship. Questioning my faith and the Catholic Church screwed up another.

Note to self: I've got to get a handle on this Faith and Belief Thing. Jesus.

Though I don't have a mate, I do have two daughters I love. Even if I have loved one more completely than the other. Heather's my constant. She keeps tabs on me. I never figured she'd wind up selling real estate but there you have it. It suits her temperament. She doesn't flaunt her money but she does love her Mercedes.

She married smart. Kyle's a good man, a loving husband and father. He's an independent sort, an artist with a camera and a water color brush. Like Renoir he's always looking for the light. He makes out okay but he's not embarrassed to admit his wife earns the real cash.

Now that I've cleared some space in my mind where I've allowed Heather to grow up, I don't mind the notion of Kyle bonking the daughter I love so much. I hope she's bonking him back. So much fun I forgot about.

I also have Olivia and Amelia. You haven't met them yet but I love them and I think they love me.

They're lively girls. They're openly interested in the world. They're beginning to think for themselves. A good thing. I worry more about them since they're driving. If you've ever handed over your car keys to your kid for the first time you know what I mean.

If I can get them to put down their phones, which they rarely do, the girls aren't too cool not to talk to me. I feel privileged to hear what they offer. The dribs and drabs they share about their lives. I've even met a boyfriend or two.

Of course I'm a boy. I know what straight boys want. I don't like the boyfriends very much. Something I'm not exactly proud of. Regardless, the girls put up with me. And I love it they ask me to take them fishing.

As long as I'm talking about my kin, you know I have to include Kirkallen and Noir. Since when has blood mattered as far as family goes? What *matters* is the heart.

Kirkallen claims I saved his life, which I did. But it's mutual. He keeps me honest and on track. I keep him on the Straight and Narrow. I'm glad he fishes.

Noir? We love to let her take care of us. We love her. We don't say it but we do. And the cool thing is now I know she loves us. I heard her say it.

So this is my life. I would've liked to do better.

It's easy to let my Failed Professional Life go. That's on me. But Abby and Elizabeth matter. They're important.

At least I've finally talked with my estranged daughter. I look forward to trying to heal our relationship. I think we will. As we do, I also need to resolve Abby's and my differences, one way or the other. We owe it ourselves. We owe it to our family.

It looks like I'm about to begin that work now. I'm still standing down on the harbor beach and the rally to save The Convent is breaking up. The sky and air are alive with a coming storm and Miss Abby and Miss Hannah are walking toward me.

The real storm might break when I speak with those two women. I wonder if Abby and Hannah know they have a common connection in *moi*.

YOU KNOW THIS MAN?

"As I live and breathe," Abby Delaney greets her husband, "I never thought you'd have the courage to grace our presence."

She greets Hardy's companions. "Noir? Why haven't you visited us? Welcome, dear. It's great to see you." They hug and Abby releases her to address Kirkallen.

"It's about time we met. You've got your hands full looking after your Resident Atheist."

It's a rare moment when Kirkallen is speechless. They shake.

Hardy attempts to respond to his wife but Hannah Penner cuts him off. "You know this man?" she asks her close friend.

"Know him? He's the father of my children." She turns to Hannah and shrugs. "Remember we agreed to leave Our Skeletons in the closet?"

"Right." Hannah pauses. "I'm surprised … that's all. You said your husband wasn't coming."

"That's what I thought."

"I'm here," Hardy interjects, hoping to deflect Hannah's direction.

He doesn't ask how he's evolved from a collegiate Exotic Temptation to a Resident Atheist and a Skeleton in a closet.

"Husband in name only," Abby counters with sarcastic emphasis.

This is getting complicated. A lot of layers here.

Heather Hardy Bartlett, family in tow, arrives to save the day.

She wears cuffed khakis and a gauzy blouse, a navy sweater looped over her shoulders. A *Bartlett Realty* ball cap holds her blonde hair in place. "Isn't this a lovely scene? I was afraid you might not talk. I do hope you're being civil. This is a festive occasion. Let's keep it that way. For Elizabeth's and Alexandra's sakes. Aside from wedding festivities we've just heard rousing words about saving a convent. I can't think of a better cause to rally 'round.

"Kyle and I and the girls are staying on after the wedding and help keep the tractors out."

She focuses on Olivia and Amelia. "Girls? Did you remember your raincoats?" She lifts her face to the darkening southern sky. "You might need them if you stay put much longer."

There's a rumble of thunder. The wind picks up, roiling the harbor and riffling their clothing. A smattering of heavy drops plops audibly.

Heather continues, "We've got wedding chores to do up on the hill. I'm getting there before I get wet."

Olivia takes the hint and seizes her aunt's arm. "Come on, Aunt Hannah, ride with us. We had a blast on our road trip. We'll tell you about it."

Hannah's relieved to be off the hook. She hasn't been asked why she asked Abby about knowing Hardy. She's content, for the moment at least, to hide Hardy's skeleton in her closet too. She permits Olivia to lead her toward the Suburban. "It sounds like I'm going to hear a version of *Mr. Toad's Wild Ride.*"

"A G-rated one," Amelia adds.

"It better be."

Kyle catches his wife's eye. He's donning rain gear. "Drive back with your dad? I want to hang on the beach." He raises his camera, "To capture the light on the water and in the clouds."

Micah Hardy's head is in the clouds. Abby doesn't know about him and Hannah.

MAKE THE MOST OF MY REMAINING TIME

I hope you don't think I was too tough on Micah at the harbor. I greeted him with harsh words because I still love him. He doesn't need to know that.

I was playing defense to hide my hurt. Not that I understand why. Maybe it's because I should've tried harder to make *Us* work. *We* should have tried harder. Neither of us knew how.

So my hurt made me sound the bitch when I met Micah. The comment about him having the courage to show up? My overall tone? That's not me. Unforgiveable. I hope the First Impression I made with you doesn't last.

Since Hannah's driving to The House with my grandchildren, I'm alone as I drive to the same place. I'll tell you my story. How I got here.

I'll try to tell it in straightforward fashion. I'll also try to keep my feelings from interfering. That won't be easy.

My name is Abigael, a Celtic name given to me by my second-generation American folks, Katie and Liam Delaney.

Pa's grandparents met in Saint Paul during their arduous emigration from Cork, Ireland, to the copper mines in Butte, Montana. A blizzard stopped their train, literally in its tracks.

They never left the Midwest. They married and made Saint Paul home. They created a family. Two generations later, there was me and Ma and Pa and Sean and Brendan and Maureen. We called ourselves *The Saint Paul Delaneys.*

Pa says we've got roots in Wicklow, south of Dublin on the Irish Sea. He claims heritage to a Leinster king in pre-Viking time.

Ma? She thinks she could find a Dublin blood connection but she can't pinpoint her heritage.

I can pinpoint mine. I'm Homegrown American. Born and reared in Saint Paul. They call me *Abby.*

During my junior year in college I did an internship semester in the Big City on the East Coast where I met a tall seminarian who was fulfilling a field work requirement at the Riverside Church. We worked side by side doing community outreach from a storefront on 125th Street, one of Harlem's main drags. I fell in love almost immediately with Micah Hardy.

I believed we could make our Interfaith Thing work. Me the Good Catholic. Him the Presbyterian Minister in Training.

I also knew a secret he didn't.

I didn't tell him I knew he'd never get ordained.

He could never be a minister. That suit never fit right. He needed more room. Still does.

I completed my internship and returned to Saint Teresa, a tiny conservative college in southern Minnesota, while Micah completed his final seminary semester.

Micah felt he was too young and too inexperienced to be a minister when he graduated. That's what he told himself—and me. It might've been his hormones doing the thinking. He wanted into my knickers something awful.

He begged one reference letter from his Southwest basketball coach and a second from a seminary professor to help him land a job at St. Rose College in Saint Paul.

To be near me.

I knew he meant business. He chose a $6K-a-year-job over an offer to earn eighteen thousand.

I'm glad he followed me home.

Micah worked in Residence Life for St. Rose and lived in a dorm. My folks lived nearby in the home Heather and Kyle bought from them. We courted in a sheltered and protected environment as I finished my senior year, commuting home almost on a weekly basis. I disappointed Ma and Pa when I decided not to go to grad school.

Because I loved Micah Hardy.

We married in June right after I finished school.

Ma and Pa acted okay about me marrying a non-Catholic because Micah didn't mind me wanting to keep my family name. Once a Delaney, always a Delaney. Pa said he could be partly happy I married a Scot-Irish boy. At least Celtic blood ran in his veins. What my folks really liked is that he agreed to go the Church of the Ascension with me and to rear our children as Catholics.

We'd barely seen each other naked when we conceived Heather. Libby came later. After we gave up on it.

Ma and Pa took absolute delight when Micah stood next to me on the altar for Heather's baptism and pledged to rear her in the Catholic tradition, which we did with her and Libby too.

Ma's dead now. I held her hand as she expired in Sisters of Mercy Hospital not far from where I used to live with Micah. Pa? He's frail and failing and living with my brother and his wife outside of Phoenix. My brother Sean despises cold weather.

A dutiful father, Micah moved from position to position at St. Rose, gaining responsibility as he progressed. Then he accepted the Government Relations gig.

The longest position he ever held was the one he hated. He detested the Corporate Doublespeak he mouthed. He mourned privately at how easily it came out, how easily he appeared to care for community values to get what St. Rose wanted.

He said he took the promotion for the salary. Even so, we could never afford our Lakeside Vacation House. Any money we accrued went to the girls' Catholic Educations.

As far as education goes I know one reason Micah kept his job. The college had a great tuition remission deal with other Catholic colleges.

There was one other reason too. We absolutely needed health insurance.

The girls weren't always easy. I had some hectic years but I'd never take back a minute of that time. I put my life into those two and when Heather left for college I felt she took a piece of me with her.

I wasn't exactly overjoyed when Heather chose the University of San Diego. California … of all places … but free tuition at a Catholic college made sense.

That is it made sense until the end of Heather's senior year when she Had to Get Married.

Kyle Bartlett. A sweet WASP of a boy. He did my girl wrong, then he did my girl right.

They didn't have a church wedding but thank the Lord Kyle took the RCIA training and converted. Having Olivia grounded them. They're loving parents and they love each other.

Libby? She went up the road to St. Benedict. That proved a problem when, as a senior home for Christmas, Micah caught her as he said *With that son of a bitch's hand up her skirt.*

He never elucidated.

I had the smarts not to ask even though I suspected Libby didn't have her skirt on.

Libby returned to school. She never came home.

It killed me they argued and fell out. Both too darn stubborn for their own good. And for mine.

Micah never apologized or reached out. The fool. I wanted to wring his neck.

Too angry—and too proud, shades of her father—Libby refused to come crawling home.

Micah didn't even attend her commencement.

After Libby went to grad school, Heather moved the remainder of her sister's things out. With Heather married and Libby gone, the house got very empty. I couldn't fill the void completely with grandmother chores so I started doing more and more for the church and the Fathers.

As my interest increased Micah's waned. He said he didn't want to join the Country Club. He said our priests were too rigid and conservative. He said anyone who refused to give communion to a non-Catholic or a homosexual didn't understand the true meaning of God's grace.

What really sealed it? Micah couldn't buy into the notion of Christ as the Exclusive Way to Salvation. There's a verse about that in John's gospel I think.

We agreed to disagree.

No. That's not accurate. We didn't talk about it.

Or Libby.

With the girls fledged and my relationship distanced I had nothing to stay for. I didn't feel needed. I didn't know if Micah wanted me.

I'd done my job, reared my girls as best I knew how. I played the steadfast wife too. For that matter I am the steadfast wife. I haven't slept with another man. I have zero interest in the act or the complications it brings.

On that score and for all his faults I don't think Micah ever cheated either. I'd rather believe that than know any other truth. It's how I can think kindly of him because as I told you I love him. I think he loves me. It's a shame we don't know how.

I easily rationalized my Exit Plan. I'd taken the balance of my life, its weight and measure, and found it lacking. I wanted … no, I needed … I felt bound to find a meaningful place in the world. I wanted to make the most of my remaining earthbound time. I decided to devote myself to a life of active faith.

I drew a line in the sand.

I can't live with man who doesn't go to church, who doesn't Believe Right.

I called him *Hardy* when I said it. I'm one of the few who calls him by his Christian name. I like the biblical feel of it on my tongue. But using his surname made me sound harsher and braver than I felt. I needed to do that too. It made it easier to leave. I pretended to take a Righteous Stance.

What I should have done is the Righteous Thing.

Stay and work it out. We owed each other that much.

We still do.

Remember what I said about Micah and Libby's stubborn ways? I can be stubborn too. I refused to do it.

I lived with a friend while I searched for work. Heather got my things from the house as necessary. That was easy. Kirkallen hadn't arrived; Noir's a late-comer. Our house was empty while Micah worked.

I got two breaks. First, a group of Benedictine nuns gave me shelter. The ever hospitable sisters, salt of the earth women, accepted me with Open Arms. I watched as they lived out their motto, *Ora y Labora*.

Pray and work.

I simplified my life. I learned to pray.

Praying in community cleared my head. Cleared my heart. I found a Deeper Faith.

I loved the beautiful simplicity of the parts of monastic living I experienced. I considered becoming an oblate. That's an associate member. But first I wanted to embrace the broader world.

I landed a meaningful position with Catholic Charities. Then I discovered my First Cause. I led a women's coalition and we established a home for battered women in a neighborhood that didn't welcome us with open arms.

Now they do.

Then Libby told me she visited a friend in Cedar Harbor and how she liked the look of the retreat center up there. I checked it out and rented a room for a week at The Convent of Holy Sisters and met Hannah Penner. Hannah the Mennonite.

We hit it off and started working together. Doing what we love—talking with our sisters about the Christian Life, about the meaning and value of service, about what it means to be a spiritual person. You know we launched an interfaith personal retreat enterprise that turned a tidy profit before spiraling out of control.

Thank God we got out of the business. You know we sold it, moved to The House on the Hill and invested in The Convent of the Holy Sisters.

I found my life there.

I love my daughters. I love my grandchildren. I love Kyle. I love Alexandra. I love Hannah and her daughter too.

I also love my Cedar Harbor Life. I love serving as an alderwoman. I love making The Convent viable. I love the work we do. We hold fast to a John Wesley saying.

"Do all the good you can. By all the means you can. In all the ways you can. In all the places you can. At all the times you can. To all the people you can. As long as you ever can."

That brings you pretty much up to speed. The Lord has proved sufficient for me until this day. I know not to ask for more.

Going forward we'll put up the Good Fight. Though I will work to save The Convent I will accept the Lord's Plan if we don't. We'll take the temperature of that struggle beginning Monday.

Right this moment I have my little girl's wedding to attend to. Thank goodness Marion is in firm control. Especially since there's a variable I haven't considered. It's going to be more complicated than I thought. I don't know exactly what I'm feeling about Micah being here. I didn't think he was coming. My daughters didn't tell me anything different. But then again I don't remember asking.

I think I wanted to avoid thinking about him coming so I assumed he wasn't. I do know I told Hannah the wedding was going to be less of a hassle for me and Elizabeth because he didn't want to attend.

It also appears I have an additional Awkward Variable to deal with.

Hannah seems to know Micah. You heard her. She said *You know this man?* I wonder what that's about.

THIS TAKES THE CAKE

The drive to The House feels tense.

Kirkallen and Noir and I feel tense because we heard Hannah ask Abby if she knew me and we saw Hannah's mouth drop open when she heard Abby's response. So because Heather butted in, the rains came and the girls whisked Hannah away, we're guessing that Abby doesn't know what Hannah just discovered.

How I'm connected to their lives.

Meanwhile Heather's stiff as a poker. She's riding shotgun with Muskie curled in her lap. She's not talking because we're not talking. The question I'm considering is if she doesn't know about Hannah and me why did she commandeer the conversation at the harbor? Maybe she's got great ESP and sensed the awkwardness? Who knows what she knows?

I don't know how to ask that question.

I do know this. I know Heather knows Hannah and likes her. Apparently Heather's children love her. They call her *Aunt Hannah.*

I also know Heather doesn't say it to her mom but she's delighted Abby's found a solid reliable friend in Hannah.

They make a good pair. Business partners. Soul mates. They do good work. They've found the right places to be. The right persons to be. What a blessing.

I am jealous.

But my jealousy takes a back seat to my utter discombobulation.

As we reach the clearing at the top of the drive a dramatic bolt of lightning illuminates the sky, momentarily shivering as it spears into the pewter and frothing lake.

"Better get inside and beat the rain," says Heather stiffly. "I'm heading over to the cabin to check in with the girls."

She's gone in a flash. Doesn't even say goodnight.

I ask Kirkallen and Noir to sit on the veranda and watch the storm. What I'm saying is I need to talk. This is the New Me.

"I'll fetch the pipe." Kirkallen trots toward our cabin.

He returns as Noir and I are setting the pansy baskets against the house wall, out of the wind. The decorative bunting crackles but it's tied tight.

We push the chairs out of the blowing rain. The town below is hidden under gray cloud. We stare over a sea of mist through which one Lutheran church steeple emerges. The very sanctuary Robert Kerr commissioned, though an influx of Scandinavian settlers altered its natal Presbyterian allegiance.

Muskie doesn't hesitate. She proceeds deliberately to the empty glider and curls up on half. It's moving of its own accord. What's with that?

I start talking.

I can't believe this situation I tell my friends. I tell them this takes the cake. My other complications are child's play.

Losing my job? What a gift.

My lesbian daughter? So what? She's talking to me.

A same-sex wedding? It's legal. They're in love.

The Convent controversy? That's life in a small town and we're outsiders.

But this Hannah and Abby Thing? My head's spinning. I don't know what to think. Let alone feel or do. I ask my friends, "Got any ideas?"

No one replies.

We watch the storm. Lightning flashes and crackles over the lake. Thunder booms.

I decide not to relate my Thunderstorm Memory as it pertains to my evening with Hannah Penner.

"We have an open day tomorrow. The wedding's not 'til Saturday," Kirkallen muses. "I saw a canoe hanging from the carriage house rafters. This weather's supposed to clear out. Let's go fishing."

"Let's."

Noir stands and stretches. "Time for bed," she says through a yawn. "I've had a long day." She casts a critical eye on Hardy. "And if I've had a long day, I suspect yours has felt longer. You did run into your fair share of surprises."

"True enough," Hardy agrees.

"And," she concludes, "I'm guessing one of the many things you didn't expect to encounter at this wedding is you'd be the one needing an emotional break in the action. A psychologist might say you need a Corrective Emotional Experience."

"And that's fishing?" Hardy ventures.

"And that's fishing."

HELPING ME SORT THINGS OUT

It's not unusual to wake before dawn. Neither of us sleeps soundly. An old man's malady. Besides there's The Fishing. We like to think we're good at it but are content with liking to do it.

We're moving circumspectly in the dim light. Trying not to disturb the others. Muskie straggles out from Noir's cabin while we secure the canoe to the Forester. She performs her Downward Dog pose. Then she pees and I get to feeling wistful. What I'd really like is to live in a place where I can get up, walk outside, stretch and take a whiz on solid earth.

"Muskie's abandoned Noir's warm bed?" Kirkallen observes as she jumps into the back seat. "We should be flattered."

He shakes his head. He's thinking faraway thoughts. Maybe about missing sharing a bed with a Favorite Other. He unconsciously adjusts the white garter on his upper left biceps.

"You rather sleep with a chick or go fishing?"

There's no need to answer. I yearn for the days when Abby and I used to screw each other silly. What ever happened to Us anyway?

"We do have this." Kirkallen produces a thin one, lights it, inhales and hands it over. "May as well see The Magic."

We're fishing this morning ostensibly to give me a break from my confusions. Space to consider the recent disclosures and surprising discoveries. Though we've vetted the details of that song and dance I still wonder what will happen if my wife knows I *knew* Hannah biblically.

Jesus.

How can a simple outdoor wedding be packed with a continuing series of personal challenges and revelations? I hope I've seen the end of them.

This is where I'm supposed to talk to Kirkallen. I'm supposed to tell him how I feel and give him time to tell me whatever he needs to.

We know that's not happening. I can handle only so much of being this New Me. I'm reverting to the Old Me.

We'll talk by not talking about it directly.

We'll refer to thoughts and feelings obliquely as men do and women don't.

Mostly we're going fishing.

I inhale and exhale and see The Magic as we knife up the ridge through mists left over from last night's storm. Our headlights transform wisps of fog into phantasms.

We wind into the heart of a national forest—spruce and oak and birch and cedar and aspen and pine, interspersed among a maze of lakes and connecting creeks. Beautiful country.

Some exposed rock is older than time. Laid in place roughly two thousand million years before the present. Precambrian. What geologists call *deep time.*

It's a deep thought.

Comforting. Makes My Current Issues sound ridiculous.

The pot is working.

We cross the Laurentian Divide momentarily clearing the mist and once again descend into its grasp. Kirkallen's holding the map. "Turn right." He points. "Here. Not too far."

We bump down a two-track, park in a clearing by the water and unload the canoe and string our rods, reverently respecting the church like hush.

I take the stern seat and we push off. Muskie budges against my knees. She sits alert and examines the lifting fog.

We take a seven hard strokes and glide on dead calm black water in utter silence. Hints of orange and rose tinge the low-lying clouds in the eastern sky.

"Like we're actors in a Homer water color," Kirkallen remarks.

A loon voices a distant plaintive call. It's not possible to describe how lonesome it sounds.

Kirkallen raises his paddle clanking it against the gunnel. A harsh sound amplified by its opposite. The quiet. He points to a bald eagle perched atop a dead and spindly white pine. "We've got company."

I suggest a strategy. "Tie on a black bugger? Cast out, paddle and troll it behind us?"

"Mmm … we could. I'd rather fish dry. Let's cruise slowly and watch for circles and risers."

"We have a plan."

"See any fish?" Kirkallen asks the eagle.

A trout breaks the surface. Another swirls, chasing a meal at the top of the water column. Pretty soon we're into a rise and the bothers of our lives vanish. "Try a #12 Adams," I suggest.

I am content to paddle and put my buddy over rising trout. I steer toward a grouping of expanding ringlets.

In a matter of minutes Kirkallen comes tight to a fish. Judging by the singing reel and the arc in his five-weight Sage it's a fine one. He determinedly plays the protesting trout.

The eagle's on us in a heartbeat. She swoops low. Sharp shrieks, sharp claws and a sharper curved beak. So close her blue-black feathers shine. I hear her wings push air. See the gleam in an atavistic eye.

"Jesus! Play the fish. I'll deal with the bird." I helicopter my paddle, pushing my own air, more in self-defense than an attempt to ward off the poaching bird. I don't swear nearly as much as I used to. I do now. "Get out of here you fucker!"

My voice reverberates. It spooks us but the raptor peels away, defeated. She resumes her pine top vigil. "Go catch your own fish," I admonish.

The action focuses on Kirkallen and he deftly nets a brilliantly hued rainbow. He turns to me. "Nice work with the eagle, bro." He proudly displays his catch. "About eighteen inches, you think?"

"Yup. Nice work you. A lovely trout."

The only time guys say *lovely* to each other is when they describe a fish.

"Make a fine supper for you and me and Noir if we were going home. We can however go back to The House on the Hill and tell them we caught fish." He returns the trout to its home.

"Check it out," I say through a laugh. "Under your seat. Our brave hound."

In the excited moments, Muskie crawled forward beneath the middle thwart and tucked her head beneath Kirkallen's cane seat.

"I didn't want any piece of that eagle either." Kirkallen affectionately scratches the dog's head.

We continue our deliberate cruise and Kirkallen catches a half dozen more but nothing as big as the first. Gradually a peace and ease settle over me. A quiet contentment that soothes and clears my muddled mind.

The sun clears the tree tops. A light breeze corrugates the water. I angle our bow toward the landing. We beach the boat, break down the rods, load the canoe and store our gear while Muskie cavorts at the water's edge.

Afterward we perch contentedly under the Subaru's open hatch. Gatorades from the cooler taste good in a setting where even Gatorade can taste good. As do hard boiled eggs and slices off a block of extra sharp cheddar.

"Head back to reality?" Kirkallen asks casually.

"A great float," I offer. "Thanks for helping me sort things out."

Sort things out? It sounds preposterous but I mean it.

Talking honestly about feelings and emotions can only go so far among men. It takes the girls to make that happen. I got what I needed. Quiet time on the water with Kirkallen and Muskie.

"As far as I'm concerned we'll let the stories at The House on the Hill play out. I'll go with the flow, tell no lies and accept what happens. That will have to suffice."

On the drive home I steer into a ridgeline overlook to appreciate the dramatic sweep of Lake Superior. A brisk wind pushes the lake from out of the southeast rumpling the steely water. Farther out the sun and clouds sketch a moving vista of light and shadow. We admire our eagle eye view of the town.

I'm tempted to say how I detest Our Urban Life Style but let it slide. I offer an alternate spin. "Sure beats City Living."

Kirkallen agrees. "I could live up here. Even though I haven't seen another Brother ... except for Marion." He's distracted by the sight of a line of outsized yellow vehicles parked nose-to-tail in the public lot by the marina.

"You think they're here to raze The Convent?" he muses.

SIX

THE NUPTIALS

"MY NAME IS FOR MY FRIENDS"

The wedding party assembles under the tent for the Friday evening rehearsal and they walk through the ceremony basics. The air is scented with blooming lilac. Hardy is observing from his cottage porch.

Grace is in charge. It's obvious she's Hannah's daughter. Her confidence shows. It shines in her face. She wears a pale blue tee appliquéd with a pair of fried eggs on the chest. Like she's emphasizing her minimal bosom. Something stirs a distant memory Hardy can't quite identify.

He lets the moment pass.

The faces are familiar to Hardy. Except the Englishman and his friends.

Peter Blackstone professes music at a private college for smart rich kids. He's short and powerfully built. His hands are beautiful. Long-fingered and graceful. His eyes sparkle.

Blackstone plays a mean classical guitar as the dry run unfolds. He's brought friends. A couple who accompanied him on the Long Drive North. Fenton Carmody is tall and gangly. Like Hardy. Hardy thinks he knows him from somewhere he can't quite place. Carmody's wife is beautiful. Susannah Applegate moves with a dancer's light-footed elegance. Her long auburn hair is attractively streaked with silver.

When Grace closes the session with prayer Hannah turns to catch Hardy's eye. She beckons him as she tugs Grace and Abby by their elbows. The trio heads toward him.

Hardy's not a praying man. He feels it's too selfish to bother the alleged Almighty with petty concerns in a world where people are starving and arguing and shooting each other and poisoning the earth and melting the polar caps.

He thinks he should be praying now.

He takes a deep breath and prepares to deal with whatever's on Hannah's mind, which judging by her appearance is Something even if I, your Narrator, don't have the foggiest.

In that moment a line of iron gray SUVs approaches the stately residence and circles the drive. The motorists shut down their engines.

Muskie charges off her porch glider. She barks furiously and skids to a halt in front of the lead vehicle's passenger door.

"What's gotten into that hound?" Noir emerges from her cottage. She summons her charge who refuses to obey. She jogs to Muskie's side and grips the growling canine's collar.

It is the sole action in the lens.

No one moves. No one exits a vehicle. There's a pregnant pause as if actors are awaiting cues.

A window glides silently down.

"Keep ahold of that damn dog," Mayor Karvonen sputters.

His face is ruddy. He wears an uncomfortable frown. His demeanor suggests he'd rather be almost anywhere than in an SUV in front of The House on the Hill. He tries a more controlled tone. "We're friendly. We mean no harm."

Noir challenges the mayor. "I'm getting a negative vibe here. I've got the dog but we're not moving."

Alexandra places a light restraining hand on her friend's forearm. "I'll handle this, sweet thing," she says calmly.

To the open window she says, "Good evening, Mr. Mayor. To what do we owe the pleasure of your visit?"

"My friends and I ..." he motions to the SUVs, their cooling engines ticking in the evening air, "... we want to offer our best wishes. We hope the wedding tomorrow goes off without a hitch. We'll be here … to make sure there won't be any trouble. You know, with the same-sex thing … our more conservative and traditional residents might take offense. They could come calling."

Elizabeth Hardy joins her mate. "We're not at all concerned. We'll be among friends."

"My friends here," the mayor explains, "they've come up from the Cities to be on hand as we begin demolition on Monday. I've asked them to provide wedding security at no charge to you. Consider it a courtesy, the town's wedding gift. No need to worry. We'll stay out of the way."

The Southern lilt disappears from Alexandra's voice and she states each word succinctly. "Let me make this clear, Mayor Karvonen, you're not welcome. Today or tomorrow. Your presence now feels like a threat. What are you getting out of razing The Convent?"

"The promise of a business boost. Economic prosperity. I've struck a good deal in behalf of my constituents."

"Anything go into your pocket besides a new set of truck keys?" Elizabeth asks.

The mayor sputters at the allegation as Elizabeth continues, "Please leave. Immediately. Don't come back. I presume we'll see you at The Convent on Monday?"

"You so much as put a foot outside of that truck and I let this dog go," Noir says evenly.

Muskie underscores her mistress' intent with a growl.

Karvonen challenges Noir. "Who are you, Girl in Black?"

"My name is for my friends," Noir asserts.

It's a line from *Lawrence of Arabia*. Peter O'Toole used it while standing alone by a desert well when he first encountered Omar Sharif.

Alexandra flashes a huge smile. She loops her arm over Elizabeth's shoulder. "And this rehearsal is for my friends," she says softly. "Now please drive back down the hill. Y'all have a pleasant good night. Just don't have it here."

Later that evening in town the men who trailered the heavy equipment from the Cities—front end loaders, backhoes set on caterpillar treads, tractors and dozers—decide to drink a few beers at Superior Brewing.

Sorry, they hear. *We regret we have to close early. Our tap lines are fouled. You drink one of our beers you might get sick. We don't want that.*

The brewery owners do not invite the men to return.

WE'RE THINKING THIS NEVER HAPPENED

'Round midnight Alexandra, Elizabeth, the wedding party ladies and assorted family women drive down the hill to the brewery. The group—including Abby and Hannah, Grace, Heather and her girls, Noir, Marion and Susannah—debarks excitedly behind the brew pub.

Milwaukee and his wife, Violet, admit them through a rear door and they join a cluster of women, including the other Sisters, who've gathered expectantly. The brewers greet their guests graciously.

"I understand this might be more than a Bachelorette Thing?" Milwaukee queries. "Perhaps you're conducting some business? We closed early so you could. In private." He purses his lips as if thinking to say more.

"We got rid of a pack of undesirables for you," Violet adds. "We didn't think you'd want the demolition guys overhearing anything you might not want to share."

She dismisses her husband, "You have paper work to take care of? In the office?"

To the ladies she inquires, "May I join you? I'd like to help."

Abby and Hannah are acutely conscious of the Unsettled Questions between them. The ones they've studiously avoided discussing over the last several hours. They know this is neither the time nor the place.

There's a convent to save. Business to conduct.

They address it with conspiratorial mutterings about Karvonen, the heavy equipment, DSG, David Shire and The Convent. Conversation is punctuated with choruses of *amens*. One Sister blurts, "Our shirts?"

"Not my girls," Heather says firmly to which one of hers splutters, "Mom?"

It doesn't take long.

The women are on point, focused. They set a course they are determined to navigate. Grace closes with prayer. They ask for strength, guidance, unity of purpose.

Even Noir closes her eyes.

The mood lightens when Violet moves behind the taps. "I'd like to toast the happy couple," which she does in an eloquent fashion, finishing with, "Beer's on the house but for anyone wanting a Lighter Little Something there's birch beer and spring water in the fridge."

The toast is Milwaukee's cue. He emerges with three trays piled with crackers, cheeses, dips, crudités, smoked fish and charcuterie.

There's no need for Milwaukee to attract the group's attention. The food served that purpose. His tone is reassuring. "As far as Violet and I are concerned, ladies? Whatever meeting you might have had—as well as whatever happens here tonight? We're thinking this never happened." He bows to a round of mild applause and indicates a box of Superior Brewing tee shirts on the bar. "Feel free to take one when you leave tonight."

Milwaukee departs and the women are once more left to their own devices.

Women without men. They are pleased to be present. To celebrate a Common Sisterhood. To snack, converse openly and quaff *gratis* pints.

Heather smiles broadly as Olivia and Amelia take it in. With eyes and ears wide open they discover how it is women comfortably relate to other women.

Everyone—I mean everyone—is talking with her hands. You'd think you were in a room full of Italians.

The ladies get to toasting.

Some are heartfelt and eyes get misty.

Some are plain ribald.

Then the minister offers an irreverent salute which her mother shrugs off with a wry smile.

Noir uncharacteristically chats up a storm. She can't remember the last time she enjoyed herself so completely and felt so completely at ease.

IT'S AN IDLE CONSIDERATION

While the women conspire and toast, Kirkallen and Hardy toke from a sacred Catlinite pipe and sip their Balvenie on the front porch of The House on the Hill. Kirkallen stands to retrieve a piece of pottery.

"I bought this at an art gallery in town. The *only* art gallery in town. It has a Scandinavian name."

He lights a Moroccan Scent Altar and places a small dish of fragrance over it. The heat produces a cedar bouquet that is carried along by sweet lake air.

Muskie's favored glider is empty and motionless. The boys wonder aloud where the dog's gone to but it's an idle consideration. "Probably with Noir," Kirkallen comments.

"Dog's more hers than mine." Hardy is not troubled by the notion. "Noir needs Muskie. Muskie needs Noir."

Feet on the rail, they nestle under cotton quilts and consider the lake. Silently they track a freighter churning steadily away from Duluth.

Summer stars loom above the southern horizon. Scorpio and the Teapot. The Teaspoon of Sagittarius. Higher up the Northern Crown blends into the Milky Way, an obvious bright smudge thumbed on a dark background.

Kirkallen yawns as he ponders the heavens and its billions of distant suns. "The *Dineh* believe the stars in the Milky Way are the footprints of their spiritual ancestors."

As Kirkallen drifts away, snoring lightly, Hardy briefly wonders about the Unvoiced Issue between Abby and Hannah. The one involving him. He's content to let them take it Off Pause in due time.

That's what a fishing trip and talking with a friend can do for you.

It's been a long day. Hardy doesn't realize there's much more ahead. The excitement's not over yet.

"I CHOOSE TO BE WITH YOU"

Noir is slightly tipsy when she returns. She takes the porch steps in an energetic bound. She rouses The Lads and begins without preamble.

"We're staying? After the wedding? We'll go to The Convent on Monday? We have to. I've already called work. Left a message about needing to take a week off to take care of important family business. It's a done deal."

Noir stares at the vacant, unmoving glider. "Where's Muskie? Where's our dog?"

Muskie takes her cue and scrambles onto the veranda to greet her friends. She's panting. Her coat is matted and damp, thick with bramble and burr.

"Where were you, girl?" Noir queries. She regards the dog as if expecting an answer.

"What's this?" Noir rubs her dog's back and displays two smeared fingers. "Oil? What'd you get into?" She extracts a kerchief from a pocket and wipes Muskie's coat.

Muskie mutters a contented *Woof* and assumes her customary place on her side of the glider. It resumes rocking.

"What's the deal with that chair?"

The boys are silent and Noir shrugs. She pulls an Adirondack into line with her guys. The beer has loosened her tongue.

"You'll be happy to know I defended your honor at the pub. The women worked me for staying with you. They said a young woman like me ought not to be living with two old reprobates. But I corrected them. I told them for all your faults you're pretty decent feminists. Besides you guys are so ancient your hormones aren't a threat to anyone, let alone me."

"Faults? What faults?" Kirkallen butts in. "And who's a reprobate?" He lets his indignation show. "I used to be. Not now."

"Truth," Noir concedes. "Good for you on the Reprobate Score. But the Faults Part? You're guys. That goes with the territory."

"I think the hops might've been talking for you at the brewery?" Hardy arches his eyebrows. "That hormone comment? Think that might have been too much info? You know Abby and Libby and Heather were there? My wife and my daughters? My granddaughters too?"

He doesn't put Hannah's name on the list. Noir gushes, "There were a whole bunch of other ladies there. We had a great time." As an afterthought she addresses her more personal comment. "Maybe I should've held off on the hormones. But," she continues stubbornly, "it's true. I don't see any women traipsing in and out of our place. Except for Heather and her girls."

The trio laughs and lapses into companionable taciturnity. Noir finally yawns. She stands and stretches. She's aware The Lads are ogling as her breasts test her sweater material. "I'm fading. I need to crash. Before I do let's get one thing straight about me living with you." She holds a beat of silence to emphasize what's coming. "I like it. I like it a lot. Even when you scope my chest, which you both just did.

"'I'm with you because I choose to be with you. I don't want to live someone else's idea of how to live.'" She pauses again. "That's from Redford. *Out of Africa.*"

"I wish I had your balls," Hardy says simply. "I need to take that How to Live Notion to heart."

Noir thinks a moment. "Funny. When I laid that Redford line on the ladies at the brewery a couple of them said the same thing."

"Amen," Kirkallen intones.

A FRIEND TO WALK THROUGH LIFE WITH

It's early. Not quite six. I'm alone and sipping coffee on The House porch. It's quiet save the *Who Cooks for You* hoot of what Hardy tells me is a Barred owl. Muskie's sleeping beside me on the glider. She's oblivious to the peace I'm finding. As are The Lads. I've checked on them. Hardy and Kirky are sawing serious lumber in their cottage.

I hear footsteps upstairs. People are stirring. There's a wedding today. For the present I'm happy to have the time to reflect.

There's a ton of light in the sky. So much more than in the Cities. It's the light that woke me. That and the Energy Field buzzing inside me.

Sure I got a little buzzed on the beers last night. Maybe I did share a little too much information but I got more wired by the Estrogenic Energy in the brewery. It's contagious. I can't remember when I had that much fun.

I'm not much good at being in All Female Company. So this was extra special. Not once did I fret about someone asking me why I wear black.

Even better I've joined A Cause. I'm going to stand with The Convent Women. Stand against DSG. Stand against Development. We'll stand together Monday—after today's festivities and tomorrow's recovery.

I think the wedding's where this tale was supposed to go and finish. I'm not sure why or how it's finding its own direction, regardless of where the various storytellers think they're taking it. So at this point I bet you're like me. You're wondering not only about the wedding and about what will happen with Abby and Hannah and Hardy but also about what's going to happen at The Convent.

That can wait. You'll have to be patient. For now I don't want to lose my thread. There are things I need to say.

I'll lead with the narrators.

It's obvious the primary ones are male. All you have to do is listen.

Even if they don't get it they're subconsciously sexist. Like they frequently focus on women's chests. When it comes to describing someone's appearance or what a person is wearing? The narrators are checking the women out. Their individual topographies. We're who they look at most. We're the ones they dress up. So they can take our clothes off.

Aside from mentioning Hardy's sensible Merrell footwear, a brief reference to Kirkallen's standard attire, the casual mention of fishing shirts or Celtic sweaters and the fact that someone will have to describe Kirkallen's distinctive wedding garb, all references to clothes are pretty much when women are wearing them.

Next—and even Abby and I have fallen short—no one's gotten to the guts of the matter, though I admit Hardy's making a good go at it. But that beer last night sure helped. I'm going to relate some of the personal stories the women shared at the pub. Things people generally don't admit. I'll tell you where they're human. Most vulnerable.

Take Grace. She's cool. For a minister I mean. I could actually talk to her and feel comfortable. Be myself. Strange, because I'm so not like her. She's an innocent. Reared a conservative Mennonite, she attended a Mennonite college and seminary. She admits in her toast since her church doesn't endorse same sex relationships or marriage she grew up assuming all gays and lesbians were sinful. She tells us she'd never met a lesbian. And that right there shows you how completely clueless she used to be. I bet she had a gay roommate and didn't know it.

Then she meets two lesbians. Elizabeth and Alexandra. She learns to love them. Actually figures out they're gay before they tell her. Her mind broadens when she realizes she's got Lesbian Friends She Loves. Lesbian Friends who are Children of God.

She says their friendship made a huge difference in her life. Made her more accepting. Like a good minister ought to. So she thanks Alexandra and Elizabeth. Gets teary about it. She says she owes them.

Later today Grace is putting her ministerial license on the line. By doing the wedding she officially places herself, how'd she say it? *At variance with church doctrine.* They could give her the hook or do whatever they do to un-minister somebody.

Whatever else you think, you have to admire Grace for Doing What She Thinks Is Right. What she thinks God thinks she ought to do. Not what some church says she should or shouldn't.

Then there's Abby. The totally conservative Catholic stay-at-home mom. The staunch defender of The Church of Rome. She stands and lifts a glass and confesses how much it hurt to hear her daughter Come Out.

Abby says she prayed for guidance. She thanks Hannah for helping her work through her confusions and she credits God for helping her understand how good it is for people to love and be loved.

Her toast is beautiful. Especially because it's so poignant. She admits to her own loneliness. She misses being in a Complete Relationship. She tells Elizabeth and Alexandra how happy she is they've found a good friend to walk through life with. How lucky they are.

I get misty when I tell you this today. Partly because that's exactly what I need.

A friend to walk through life with.

I hope Abby finds a friend too. I think she loves Hardy. I think Hardy loves her. And if they can work that out and get back together … well … I hope me and Kirkallen will have a place to stay.

Heather says Libby's sexual preference hasn't and won't affect their relationship. They're sisters and the love each other. She has two issues. First there's Libby and her dad. She hopes they can love again. She hopes the same for her parents. That makes her mom cry.

Hannah? She's the quiet one.

She's terribly lonely. She never had a friend to walk through life with. At least she's got a piece of Abby.

I haven't told anyone what I've figured out. Hannah's deepest darkest secret is the source of her greatest joy.

Hannah says since Grace is grown and lives nearby she hopes they can walk through life together as friends. If they find Significant Others? She says she hopes Beautiful Grace wins that race.

So like my friend Hardy says, *There you have it.* Truths that Beer Brings Out.

And how weird is it I absolutely loved hanging out with all these Religious Ladies who wear their faith on their sleeves?

DSG Go Home.

SOMETHING'S FISHY

The wedding women are lounging on the porch. They're marshaling their energy for the special day and nibbling croissants and sipping coffee when, just after eight, the mayor approaches. He's driving his new Silverado 1500.

Karvonen motors his window down and leans out. He's checking for Muskie. "Where's that damn dog?" he queries.

"If she were here she'd be barking," Abby answers. "She owns a nose for negative energy."

Hannah the Mennonite adds, "I'm not a fan of intimidating others but, in this case, I don't have a problem with you being afraid of a forty pound dog."

"There's been trouble at the harbor," the mayor states. "Someone tried to disable the machinery parked in the marina lot but I think we can fix it and stay on schedule. Though no real harm's done there is malicious intent."

"And you think we know something? That's not our style." Alexandra's offended.

Abby sounds tougher than she feels. "We wouldn't resort to below the belt tactics. We'll find a legal way to stop you."

The mayor says, "We thought we might have a problem so we rigged remote cameras to the light poles. We couldn't see anything on the recording."

He considers his choice of words and offers a correction. "What I mean is we didn't see any *people* in the video. All we saw was that miserable hound … prancing around the equipment, wagging her tail like her butt would fall off. Then she runs away. Takes off like a shot, chasing something we can't see."

"Muskie?" Abby says. "Noir's getting dressed in her cottage. I suppose Muskie's with her. She usually is. I don't know where she was last night but you didn't see her do any damage, did you?"

"No. The video is weird. It's like the dog's watching somebody. Somebody we can't see."

"You've come to tell us you captured a dog on video doing nothing but wagging her tail? Is that it?" Alexandra asks.

The mayor averts his eyes and does not comment.

"Muskie's been keeping that glider company since she got here." Elizabeth is thoughtful. "You think she's seeing something? Or somebody?"

"Maybe the ghost of Robert Kerr?" Alexandra suggests. "My relative who donated the lumber and the labor to build The Convent. Maybe his ghost isn't happy about DSG's plans."

"I bet it's the ghosts of his daughters. They were sassier." Elizabeth is fond of sassy women.

"Mayor Karvonen, are you telling us ghosts damaged the equipment?" Abby asks. "Sounds a shade far-fetched, don't you agree?"

"No spirit pulled those wires," the mayor scoffs. "Something's fishy and I'm thinking you know something about it."

"Not us," the women chorus.

"Right ... I'll leave it there and we'll fix the equipment. See you at the wedding."

The mayor closes his window. As he circles the drive and steers down the hill the group breaks into collective laughter.

There's a sticker affixed to the Chevy's tail gate.

Save The Convent.

BOUND TO ONE ANOTHER IN A HOLY COVENANT

You ever go to a wedding that isn't beautiful? This one is too.

Folks dress in what passes for their idea of finery. Alexandra wears a 1940s-vintage pale green swing dress, a knee-length item that flows and ripples with the breeze as she moves.

Elizabeth is resplendent in a dress she purchased at an antique clothing store, a flower patterned yellow rayon number that is gathered at the waist,

Neither wears any jewelry. Their hair is pulled back, held in place by white ribbons. The effect allows their faces to shine with undisguised delight. They clutch matching bouquets of purple iris tinged by yellow centers.

Grace wears an understated purple dress as Kirkallen predicted. She drapes a brilliant rainbow-colored scarf over her shoulders and knots it around her neck. She radiates beauty and confidence and strength.

The mothers garb themselves in appropriate fashion and uncharacteristically spend more time on their appearance than usual or necessary. They continue to avoid Their Question with small talk.

"No one's paying attention to me," Abby comments.

"Nor to me," Hannah retorts.

"Doesn't stop us from sprucing up."

Hannah provides a regretful conclusion. "We can't quite escape our Feminine Demons."

Noir is lovely in light pink. Her front pleated soft terry dress is set off by low black Converse gym shoes and short pink socks.

"You look great," Hardy says appreciatively. He's outfitted as his standard boring self.

Noir quickly brushes away the compliment with a retort from a Robert Mitchum-Kirk Douglas flick. *Out of the Past.*

"All women are wonders because they reduce men to the obvious."

Kirkallen's decked out in a cotton dashiki and matching kofia cap. Of course he's sporting his white armband. "I know I look fine," he preens.

Noir can't resist sarcasm. She paraphrases Philip Marlowe from *The Big Sleep*. "And I bet you have a Balinese dancing girl tattooed across your chest."

Kirkallen is unfazed. He's one toke into the day and he grins as he voices stony philosophical thoughts about the wedding. "I think these ladies might be on to something. Excluding us men I mean. They're better off without us. Free to enjoy a much tenderer breast and the sacred cavity of life. No need to depend on the likes of my gender and our ridiculously silly appendages ..."

Noir rolls her eyes. Her response is not a suggestion. "How about we keep that commentary to ourselves, old man? The sacred cavity of life ... give me a break."

The weather is kind and the day is clear. The view over the lake is magnificent. The surface is two-toned, deep blue and flecked with scattered gems as the water ripples out from the shore about a quarter mile where the consistency and color change to a flatter paler shade, matching the pale sky. A flock of dark low flying sea birds vectors in and out of the frame.

The crowd sits quietly under the tent in the side yard. Blackstone plays a medley of exquisitely simple Celtic tunes and finishes with a classical number by a female composer. The women process down the grassy aisle on the arms of their respective mothers and present themselves to their mutual friend, Reverend Grace Penner.

They pivot and hand their bouquets to Olivia and Amelia. The pair is dressed plainly to acknowledge their friend, Grace. They're clad in navy shifts they pulled over white dress shirts.

The wedding is typically Mennonite, charmingly unadorned. There is a welcome and a scripture reading. A traditional one taken from chapter three of Paul's letter to the faithful at Colossae in Asia Minor. It is not lost on the congregation as Grace reads with a measured voice that she gender-edits as she proceeds.

"Therefore, as God's chosen people, holy and dearly loved, clothe yourselves with compassion, kindness, humility, gentleness and patience. Bear with each other and forgive one another if any of you has a grievance against someone. Forgive as the Lord forgave you. And over all these virtues put on love, which binds them all together in perfect unity. Let the peace of Christ rule in your hearts, since as members of one body you were called to peace. And be thankful. Let the message of Christ dwell among you richly as you teach and admonish one another with all wisdom through psalms, hymns, and songs from the Spirit, singing to God with gratitude in your hearts. And whatever you do, whether in word or deed, do it all in the name of the Lord Jesus, giving thanks to God the Mother through Her."

Elizabeth and Alexandra exchange plain gold bands, symbols of their unending union. They recite straightforward vows in clear confident voices. A Monarch settles briefly, vividly orange and black, on Alexandra's wine dark hair.

Grace acknowledges their marriage. "Inasmuch as Alexandra Kerr and Elizabeth Hardy have exchanged vows of love and fidelity in the presence of God and these here gathered, I pronounce that they are bound to one another in a Holy Covenant, as long as they both shall live. Theirs is a marriage that is legal in the state and right in the eyes of our Creator."

Elizabeth and Alexandra kiss.

Each mother dabs a tear off her cheek.

Grace leads a closing song. An *a cappella* version of a lovely melodic hymn, *Will You Let Me Be Your Servant*.

Hardy's throat tightens as he sings. His eyes fill with emotional water.

Grace closes in benediction. "Walk in peace. May you dwell in the House of the Lord all the days of your lives."

Kirkallen whispers to his friends. "She makes a Psalm sound good to a Navajo. They'd be walking in beauty but it's the same idea."

"Mystics know no denomination," Noir replies cryptically.

"Hmm?" Hardy asks his friends. "Did I miss something?" He's smiling, pleased as punch. Traveling in Another Dimension.

After the pronouncement the group trails the couple as they cross the lawn. They walk behind The House and follow a narrow cedar chip path. It's lined with blooming bunchberry and terminates at the ancestral graves. The couple intones a brief prayer of thanks for inheriting The House. They vow, in the memories of those buried there, to keep it vital.

Elizabeth and Alexandra lean their iris bouquets against the sisters' headstones.

IN THE REARVIEW MIRROR

The joyful but understated wedding ceremony, pictorially documented solely by friends' cell cameras, morphs into a party under the tent and spreads to the adjoining lawns, an area ringed by blooming spirea edging a forest whose treetops are filled with birdsong.

At Marion's direction, Olivia and Amelia wander among the throng. They're carrying trays and distributing glasses of *Bérêche et Fils* Brut Reserve when the SUVs motor up the hill and circle the drive. They shut down their engines.

The mayor is not with them. At least he doesn't emerge from a vehicle. No one does.

Abby holds up her hands, as if restraining the group. "I'll handle this."

She approaches the lead vehicle and the driver's window rolls down. No one recognizes the man clad in a dark suit and white shirt and black tie.

"Thank you for coming to ensure our safety," she says to him.

She turns to the guests and announces, "Let them be. But don't offer them a thing. Not even a visit to the rest room."

In the rearview mirror Micah Hardy remembers three highlights about the wedding day.

First. He's never seen women kiss. Not like these women kissed. Not like sisters. It shouldn't surprise but it does. What he remembers is how pleased he felt in knowing that the daughter he doesn't know has found someone to love. Someone who loves her back.

He feels a twinge of jealousy.

Second. When the line of SUVs appears and parks and his bold wife says her piece, he hops Kirkallen's mountain bike and speeds down the hill where he visits the American Legion and Superior Brewing. He returns within an hour. He's seated next to his bike in the bed of Milwaukee's Ford Ranger. The truck he occupies leads a line of pickups and Blazers and Cherokees and GMCs, a menagerie of working vehicles as the locals deliver a not so subtle message to the men in the SUVs.

The dark gray vehicles slink away to the cheers of the crowd.

Milwaukee and Violet unload a fresh keg to honor the occasion.

Third. He finally talks to Hannah Penner, matching her restrained greeting with his own. They hug tentatively and converse quietly and calmly. Then Hannah motions to her daughter. To Pastor Penner.

"Grace, dear, please come over." She waves her arm and meets Hardy's gaze. "Abby may as well be in on this too." She shrugs and beckons her good friend.

Grace and Abby join them.

"Abby, I'd like you to meet my old college sweetheart. The good man you married. Grace, you've asked about your papa. He's never had a clue. I never told him. Meet your father, Micah Hardy."

To Micah she says, "I should've told you. You had a right to know. I'm sorry."

The first thought that comes into Hardy's brain is how clear and pure his daughter's skin is.

WE ALL LIVE AND LOVE IMPERFECTLY

Micah Hardy changed everything. Not because I bore and reared the child he didn't know he fathered. No. It's when he showed up at the wedding. *That* changed everything. Suddenly he stood between me and Abby. He stood between me and Grace.

It was easy to hide the truth from Grace. I didn't know how the truth about her was connected to Abby. A truth I can't bear to let come between us.

You'd be correct if you guessed I've spent the last day and a half trying, unless absolutely necessary, to be Somewhere Abby Wasn't. You've read where the Narrator referred to Hardy's turmoil as having multiple layers.

I have them in spades.

I didn't have the foggiest how to handle them. I have more than an old boyfriend in the mix with Abby and her spouse. I have her husband's child too.

Given different circumstances we probably could have addressed those issues more directly and be done with them by now.

But I didn't want to spoil my best friend's daughter's wedding.

So there. I said it.

Probably the worst way I could possibly say it.

The dam in my heart just broke. I just blurted it out.

Now I'm standing in a circle of people I love and have hurt in unimaginable ways. They're speechless. Their mouths are hanging open and their eyes are wide in surprise. Mine too.

I never thought it would come to this. Never in a million years. I didn't plan on sharing. Certainly not this way.

But with the wedding and all that love and good feeling in the air … and, well, weddings are good at tugging on heartstrings, especially if you're toting an excess load of emotional baggage like I am. The next thing I know I heard someone saying what came out of my mouth.

I didn't think Grace would ever *need* to know her father's identity. I also don't know if Abby *wants* to know but I had to tell her. She *needs* to know. I hope it doesn't affect our friendship, let alone our work at The Convent. I love her.

But now I'm standing around like we all are, not knowing what to say or how to say it or who to say it to. The moment turns into moments and it feels totally bizarre.

It turns out Grace, the youngest, is the most gracious and perhaps the wisest. She steps toward me and gives me a hug. She holds on tight.

"You've carried that weight for far too long," she says without breaking away. "I'm glad you got it out. I hope it feels good. I hope you feel relieved."

She pushes me to arm's length. She squares her feet and scrutinizes me. She's about to play mother to her mother. "I'm thinking you owe everyone here his or her own explanation and I'm thinking perhaps you ought to do that one-on-one. I think we'd all like that.

"I also know we're mature enough to carry your news quietly. For the good of the wedding we'll not broadcast this revelation, will we?" She challenges us with fierce gleaming eyes as she speaks.

"What we're doing here in this moment? We can live with and learn to deal with. We don't understand Everything but it is a Beginning. It's never as apparent as it is right now that we all live and love imperfectly. We all understand that."

Grace completes her speech by turning me toward Micah Hardy. "Mama," she suggests, "why don't you start by taking my father over to the porch and spend a few private moments with him? I'm thinking maybe he's the most surprised?"

She pushes me, gently, in his direction and I put my hand out to him, which he quietly accepts.

"Wait," Abby interjects, "I have something to say. I'm the smallest player in this whole drama but I have an important role," she says firmly. "As mother to the brides I need to make sure this Bombshell doesn't upstage Elizabeth and Alexandra's wedding party. I'm going to walk off and do that but let's first get a couple of things straight. So we all know."

She stops talking and takes a deep breath. She's organizing her thoughts. "I'll try to keep this brief. Hannah, we can work out the details between us later but, really, what is there to settle? Whatever you did and had with Micah happened well before I knew either of you. I don't see any covenant violation. I'm not troubled by that. For that matter I'm interested in how you and Micah work it out from this point forward.

"But there is One Thing I do need to know. We all need to know. We all know about Micah and me. We all know Micah and I should, in fact, act like adults and figure out Where We Are. Who We Are. We owe that to all of you. But there is an Elephant standing right in the middle of our circle. I have to ask. We have to know ..." She pauses to give her question the emphasis it deserves. "Do you still love him?"

I am silent. Then words find me.

"I love the memory of him but no, I don't love him. How could I love someone I don't even know?"

This statement is something I've never considered and I'm startled by hearing it come out of my mouth. I embellish it, "But since *we* now have Grace I want to be friends. For everyone's sake, including my own."

"We can all live with that, I think." Abby says.

Then she grabs Grace's arm and turns to leave. But she stops and reverses course and my gut buckles for fear of what she's about to say. I'm afraid it'll be hurtful.

"All this happened because we went on a retreat to a lovely convent on Lake Superior. I think God meant for our paths to cross. And God will give us strength to live with the details of Your News. That's for a later time. Now we've got a wedding party to attend and I hope we can act like nothing happened. It's going on without us and I'm thinking Grace and I would like to join in and enjoy a flute of champagne. Maybe two or three."

She holds a beat of silence and glares sternly at us. "Are we having fun yet?"

IF I COULD GET IT

I drop Micah's hand almost as soon as I realize I've grabbed it. To any outside observer it looks like we're getting acquainted as we casually stroll toward the front porch. Most don't know I'm walking with my long-ago lover. And the father of my child.

Not yet.

I place my finger on his lips. "Shh. Don't interrupt? Please? Let me tell it as completely as I can. You can talk later."

He looks calm. At least on the outside. Either that or he's shell-shocked. He says, "This should be interesting. Please proceed."

And I do.

"It was a different time then. I couldn't have married you, wouldn't have married you. I couldn't run off to New Jersey to be wife to a guy studying to be a Presbyterian minister. How would I fit in? How could I fit in?

"And yes. I knew. I knew I was fertile. I've always been regular. That night? That one night? I acted out of total selfishness in a very sinful way. A sin of selfishness. A selfish sin. Whenever I read Philippians I'm reminded I should 'do nothing from selfishness or empty conceit.' It haunts me. But I love my Grace. She's a gift from God.

"I wanted a piece of you if I could get it. I loved you so much. Or I loved you like a young woman loves a young man she doesn't truly know. How a young woman loves before she knows what love is. Or how to love.

"And this is what I thought. I thought you'd do the Right Thing if you knew the truth about My Condition. That's what we called it in that time. I knew you'd give up seminary in a heartbeat if I told you I couldn't go with you. I thought I'd always feel guilty for ruining your dream. I thought you could eventually come to hold it against me. Which I thought I could stand. But I knew I couldn't stand it if you held it against Grace. Now I can say it, *Our Grace.* I'm so glad she came out a girl.

"Me? I wasn't worried about me. I knew, even at twenty-one, I could provide a loving and supportive home for a child. I knew Mama and Papa would take me in—in spite of their embarrassment. I knew they'd do the Right Thing. I also knew they'd never hold it against me. I knew they loved their God and they'd pray for guidance to the same God I loved—and, Lord forgive me, still do.

"I didn't exactly lie to them about not knowing the father. I told them I'd spent the evening with several guys late in the spring semester. That part was true. I did spend the night with several guys. You were there. We drank beers at the Prairie Schooner. Remember that bar? We sat with a gang of your guy friends. So I did spend *evenings* with them. But I didn't *sleep* with them. I let Mama and Papa assume what I wanted them to assume. What I hoped they'd assume.

"Of course today I regret not telling them. What I regret even more is not telling you. What I regret most is not telling Grace. I told myself I never really lied to her either because I never told her I didn't know her father's identity. I said her papa wasn't here so she didn't need to know.

"So I lied to myself. And, deep down, I guess Grace thinks I lied to her. She knows I hid the truth. Isn't that the same thing? I hope she doesn't hold it against me. I'll have to ask for her forgiveness. I'll have to pray about that. So will she, I expect.

"But my folks did take us in. Grace had two mothers, me and her Grandma Miriam, and one father, her Grandpa Isaac. We were a tight-knit family. And our town was a village. They pitched in too. Church and town members held their tongues and gave their love. We reared a thoughtful intelligent child and she's turned into her own good person, a lot like her father. She can tell you her story in her own good time.

"What remains for us is for me to ask for your forgiveness, to pray for forgiveness and hope that, even at this late date, you'll see this as an opportunity to get to know me and to know the daughter you never knew you had."

I WASN'T NEEDED

Hannah stops talking. She shrugs and gives me a Please Forgive Smile. In it I see a hint of the sweet collegian I once knew.

The person I think I once loved.

What do I do with Her Confession? It is a confession, isn't it? My thoughts and feelings are absolutely jumbled, racing in my brain and gut. What I say comes unbidden out of my mouth and surprises me. There's a lot of that going around.

"You're not kidding? This is happening?"

I say this because I dare not utter my initial thought.

You're sure she's mine?

She's read my mind. When she says, *Yes she's yours* and *Yes this is happening,* I say, *This is incredibly unreal,* and she says, *It is so incredibly unreal, it's real,* and I say, *That's what I get? 'I should've told you? You had a right to know?'* And she says, *I said I was sorry and I meant it* and once more asks forgiveness.

Then she considers the wedding party. She's got more explaining ahead of her and, momentarily, I understand how much more difficult this is for her than me. She has to talk to Abby and Grace. She *needs* to talk to Abby and Grace. We can talk later. After I've had time to think things through. I could say something now that might make the situation even more disconcerting.

I'm sort of listening to her rationalizations for Giving Me Time to Process while I'm remembering Our Night.

Yeah that night. I'm trying not to think about it but there you have it. The lightning two nights ago restored that vision to my conscious mind. In a flash.

It's a distant memory far more idealized, romanticized, than accurate. Hannah's lithe and unclothed body illuminated in a vivid firebolt. Like visiting the Louvre.

She's not that person anymore.

As my mind continues rapid data processing I'm wondering if there's a piece to Hannah's Truth she's not sharing?

Did she have an ulterior motive?

Did she want a baby and not want me?

How's that for Male Pride? I'm thinking like a guy. I'm taking it like most guys would.

The only person I can think of is Me.

My next thought is completely vain and self-centered.

Hannah didn't need me.

I'm staggered by the revelation.

I need to get used to the idea. I wasn't needed. Patently obvious. Just like Abby stopped needing me too.

Hannah's correct. I need to process. I don't want to put my foot in my mouth.

How'd you like it if you just found out you had a daughter you haven't known about for more than forty years? And how'd you like it if you found out about this daughter at the same time and in the same place she found out the same thing? And how'd you like it if you found out about your Love Child at the same time your wife found out you'd produced her with her best friend?

See what I mean?

After Hannah walks off to mend other emotional fences, I seek out my buddies—Noir and Kirkallen. I can't honor Grace's directive. I can't deal with this on my own. Keeping my mouth shut doesn't mean

I can't tell Kirkallen and Noir. I know my friends won't blab and my indignation's getting the best of me. I'm ready to tell them how pissed I am at Hannah.

I relate the basic plot and finish with an exasperated, "She said I had a right to know and she's sorry? That's all I get?"

Kirkallen can be direct when he needs to. He is now. His *hozro* kicks in. He doesn't hesitate. "Let your pride go, man. Get over it. It's your weekend for getting gifts. You've gotten another wonderful one. First, you've talked with Libby. Then you just acquired a daughter by marriage. Her name's Alexandra. Now she's your daughter-in-law. Third, you've gotten the best gift possible. You have another daughter. Grace is a good woman. A competent and beautiful woman. You can thank her mother for that. Even better, Grace seems to like you. You've got the rest of your life to share with her."

He sees I'm softening, coming into focus. He continues. "Consider, by my count, you basically have a whole slew of girls to care about."

"And worry about," Noir interjects.

Kirkallen enumerates my Cares and Worries on his fingers as he names them. "Heather. Olivia. Amelia. Elizabeth and Alexandra. Noir. And now Grace. Not to mention the most obvious pair. Abby and Hannah. Dig it. It's all good, my brother. You are a rich man."

When Noir suggests *We can add a housemate too*, I offer an empty look.

"Yeah," she continues, "Grace is renting in the Cities. I haven't heard her talk about a roommate or a boyfriend. Or girlfriend for that matter. I'm inviting Grace to move in with us."

I LIKE THE IDEA OF THAT

Grace and I walk away from Hannah and Micah and accept champagne from Olivia's tray. We need to talk and it's my job to initiate.

I steer Grace through the crowd toward the edge of the clearing and we stand shoulder to shoulder, facing the party. I begin with a compliment.

"You were wonderful back there. Thank you for not totally losing it. You had a right to. Your mama didn't exactly use a textbook method for sharing Her News ... Your News too."

"Aunt Abby, I'm happy to know. Finally ... I think."

I can almost hear the gears grinding in her brain, trying to connect the facts with her feelings. "I won't ask how you feel yet. You need to process. But don't be too hard on your mama, okay? She needs your love more than ever. And maybe your mom needing *our* love will help you understand my reaction too. Why I didn't lose it either. You do realize my best friend just told me she had you with my husband?

"I can't feel real anger toward Hannah. She was a blessing to me when I absolutely needed one. I felt horrified when Libby ... Elizabeth ... came out to me. Hannah helped me sort it. Helped me see how good it is for people to love. And how strange it felt for a Mennonite to remind me, a Catholic, of a primary Benedictine axiom. To forgive and to ask for forgiveness. That's when I understood I needed to ask Elizabeth to forgive me and my negative reaction. I'm grateful she did.

"So I am forgiven. I'm not sure I deserve it. In fact I know I don't. That's the beauty of God's grace. It is The Gift You Don't Deserve.

I have no qualms now about my daughter's marriage to Alexandra Kerr. It's too bad she's not Catholic but I am certain God loves them. And I loved witnessing their union today. I also loved it that you tied the knot. You did a beautiful job."

Grace reddens. "Thank you for saying that. I wanted to do a good job. As to the rest, I know we can hash out our confusions. We'll need to pray about it ..." She lapses into silence and we sip our bubbly.

"Believe it or not," she continues while avoiding eye contact, "I think this is turning into an incredibly great day. I'm delighted Elizabeth and Alexandra asked me to preside over their nuptials. The setting was perfect. I couldn't ask for a lovelier venue to do the Lord's Work. I'm also delighted to know who my father is, especially since I already know I like him ... or I like as much as I know about him."

I have to agree with Grace. "He is a good man." The sentence tastes bitter. "It's too bad ... well ... a story for a later time."

"To paraphrase Ecclesiastes," Grace begins, "there is a time and season for everything. Your relationship will work out when you guys decide to work it out. In due time.

"As for me? I'm floating. News about my father makes a perfect day more perfect. As far as I'm concerned there's more Perfect News. Something I don't think anyone's considered yet, let alone you."

I'm not sure I want to hear any more *news* today. I'm bracing for another shock when Grace says, "It's about us, Aunt Abby. If Micah's my father and you're married to him, then you're no longer a figurative aunt to me. You're sort of my stepmother, aren't you? I like the idea of that."

I haven't parsed the extent of our new and complicated relationships. I'm making the connections and Grace makes another for me. "And think about it. I just officiated at my half-sister's wedding. I like the idea of that too."

We turn and face each other. We smile and clink glasses.

A CABAL IS PLAYING OUT

This is your Narrator. I've returned to advance the plot. I haven't had to talk much lately. The story's gotten hijacked by the characters I created. They're finding their voices and I'm losing mine. Perhaps it's as it should be. What you need to know in the here and now is a cabal is playing out. Watch and listen with me.

Hardy's shakily managing his recent emotional uptilt. He's rejoining the party but the wiring's largely disconnected between his thoughts and words. He takes a vacant seat at a table with Noir and Kirkallen and Blackstone, the guitarist, and his friends, Susannah and Fenton. Their heads are bent together. They're talking earnestly.

They're plotting.

Blackstone's loosened his black bow tie. He unconsciously removes a folded piece of sandpaper from his breast pocket and smooths the nails of his right hand. It's special order stuff. He's a classical guitarist to the core.

When Hardy sits, Kirkallen looks up. He grins and points to Carmody. "Recognize this dude?"

"I know him from somewhere," Hardy comments offhandedly.

"The basketball coach. He used to coach Parker College women's hoops. His team came to St. Rose once a year. He coached some games we went to. What I remember most about Parker is the assistant coach. She was a total knockout."

"Probably the most memorable detail of my coaching career was hiring a gorgeous assistant," Carmody deadpans. He sighs, "We were never good enough to give St. Rose a decent run."

"How about we take this out of the gym and return to reality?" Susannah suggests.

She offers her hand to Hardy. "I'm Susannah. We haven't been formally introduced but I know you know my husband and I came along with Blackstone. I'm glad we did. We didn't realize when we left home that we'd be taking a longer ride. We're staying to join the protest."

A preoccupied Hardy responds more automatically than genuinely, "Glad you're here. The more the merrier."

He attempts to enter the present moment. To Blackstone he says, "You played some beautiful music. Thanks for putting the Right Touch to my daughter's wedding."

Noir calls them to task. She shushes Hardy. "We have important business. Timely stuff to finish up."

She addresses Susannah. "We're cool on this? We must initiate it here to be convincing."

"I don't know anyone here so that's your call." She adds a cryptic comment. "I've shown some skin in my time. I'm not bothered about how it'll go down."

"Fenton?" Noir asks. "You're on board?"

"Absolutely."

"We've got a good night for it," Kirkallen chimes in. "There's a new moon. There'll be very little light."

The group disbands and mixes and mingles.

Hardy dances with the brides. Then with Grace. Then Noir. Then Hannah. Then Abby.

He moves gracelessly. No surprise. For a person with decent athletic ability he owns zero rhythm. If everyone in church is clapping on beat, Hardy's clapping when they aren't. He dances like the cloddy white guy he is.

As awkwardly as he dances he *feels* ten thousand times more awkward—dancing with women he knows in completely different ways than he did a few moments ago. He likes dancing with Abby best.

It feels closer to normal than anything else.

The party continues until after midnight. Noir and Susannah are acting out. They've taken ostentatious cups from Milwaukee's donated keg. Then Noir dances especially close with Fenton Carmody. She inserts her thigh in between his during a slow number and Susannah clutches her roughly, yanks her away.

The pair squares off. The young tough woman dressed in pink glares at Susannah, her silvered auburn locks askew, her eyes on fire.

"You bitch," Susannah objects. "Keep your body off my man."

Kirkallen leaps toward the fray. "Ladies, ladies!" He wedges between them. "Easy now. Lighten up. No need for Negative Waves … what do you say we take a ride to the lake? Cool out? Walk in Beauty?"

"I'm driving," Blackstone asserts. He's pulling on a pair of light cotton gloves while he apologizes to the newlyweds. "Sorry my guest caused a ruckus. I don't know what got into her other than too much of Milwaukee's keg. I'll get everyone out of here. Ease the tension. Everything's copacetic. Dig?"

He strides to his Jeep, gets in, turns the ignition and motions to the group. "Susannah, up front with me. Noir, Kirkallen, Fenton? Squeeze in the back."

They do and Muskie leaps confidently into Noir's lap.

They drive twenty yards and Blackstone applies the brakes. Kirkallen hops out and trots over to his guest cottage. He returns with a discrete black leather case and a plastic shopping bag clanking distinctly of empty beer cans. They drive off, evidently with purpose.

No one notices except me. Everyone's having too much fun.

A GRAND ADVENTURE

Kirkallen employs an apologetic tone on the drive down the hill. "Pull to the side, please?"

"You forget to pee? An old guy with a delicate prostate?" Blackstone asks.

"Nah. I'm ..." Kirkallen loses his words. He hates to admit he's shy. He doesn't mind changing in the car in front of the others. But not in front of Noir. He can't do it. "I need to change into my work clothes."

"Change in the car," Susannah suggests. "We're on the same team."

"My wife's not very shy," Carmody clarifies. "She used to be an exotic dancer."

"Yeah, she once danced for Carmody," Blackstone offers.

Carmody gives more detail. "We weren't an item then. You can read about it in a book called *Window Dressing.*"

Noir's feeling as hesitant as Kirkallen. "I'm not wearing a bra. If I take off my dress in the car ... well ... there's a line Helen Vinson used in *The Kennel Murder Case.* It's a vintage William Powell-Mary Astor flick prior to their Thin Man Days. Helen's holding a prize show dog in her lap. She's posing for a photo opp in front a gaggle of flash bulbers and she pulls her skirt hem modestly over her knees."

"And ..." Carmody's curious about this woman who quotes old movies so readily.

"When Helen covers her knees she says, 'Sorry boys, these are not trophies.' Let's just say my ..."

"I've heard enough." Blackstone steers to the side of the dark drive.

Noir returns quicker than Kirkallen. She's pulled a slinky low-cut dress over her head. Kirkallen's dressed for action too. He's wearing black Levis, a long sleeve black tee and a watch cap. He's adjusting his white garter when he enters the car.

Carmody's been wondering. "I have to ask. What's with the armband?"

"It's a symbol of mourning I've worn since that guy who wants to Make America White Again won The Election. I'm mourning the Increased Whitening of the National Human and Political Landscape."

Susannah's changed in Noir and Kirkallen's absence. She's made a slight rip in the neckline of a tight-fitting polo dress. She shifts in her seat and holds Kirkallen's eyes with hers. "We're going to have some fun."

Kirkallen breaks into a piano key grin.

Noir recalls a phrase she used when she stood with Hardy and Kirkallen on the harbor beach at the picnic the first time Hardy saw Hannah. "Serious fun indeed," she avers. "Kirky my man, we're getting in Deeper than We Thought. This wedding is turning into a grand adventure."

IT WORKED LIKE A CHARM

All is quiet at The House on the Hill in the wake of the wedding and celebration. The air tastes clean and crisp. It smells fresh, occasionally scented by lilac wafting in from the side yard.

Ever vigilant Marion understands Hardy's become a front porch regular. She's arranged a tray on which she's placed several tumblers, an ice bucket, a decanter of malt spirits and six sweating brown bottles of Milwaukee's finest. The thoughtful hostess has set it out on a deck table and has discretely disappeared.

She's the smart one. She's in bed.

Hardy occupies a favored Adirondack and clutches a neat double. He's relaxing between his daughters. Women who are friends and have recently discovered they're half-sisters.

Heather's on Hardy's right. She's put her girls and Kyle to bed. She's pleased. She's resting a brown growler of Portage Rest in her lap. Milwaukee's decanted amber ale. She swigs from the jug.

Grace sits to the left. It's been a long day.

Conducting a same-sex wedding which puts her credentials at risk with her Mother Church.

Meeting her father for the first time.

Dancing with him.

Dealing with her confused mother.

Discovering she's got a stepmother. A couple of half-sisters too.

She's wondering how the future of her interrelated families will unfold. She's not worried. She's confident about sorting the issues in a positive manner. Good people have a way of doing that. She's not overly concerned about her church either. What will be, will be.

She nurses a light scotch and clinks the cubes as she considers the grand dimension of a night sky peppered with points of light and laden with the mystery of an unfathomable darkness.

The peaceful scene is interrupted when Blackstone pulls in front of The House. The fivesome emerges noisily from the car. They're ebullient, jubilant.

"Check out the vista," Grace greets them. "Stars galore." She gestures at the lake and sky.

Muskie charges up the steps to greet Hardy. She nuzzles him and leaps onto her glider, her tongue lolling. She circles instinctively on her customary side and settles down with a sigh.

"We've mended our fences?" Hardy queries.

"Pour me one of those?" Kirkallen points to Hardy's glass. He can't hold back. "It worked like a charm," he reports. "The Plan that is."

Noir interrupts her friend before he winds up. "I'll have a light one, like what you're pouring for Kirkallen," she says to Hardy. She drags a chair toward the porch trio and motions to Susannah and Blackstone and Carmody and Kirkallen to do the same. They form a semicircle at the rail.

Blackstone daintily removes his gloves and reaches for his sandpaper. Carmody asks for a beer and Susannah grabs a pair of bottles from the tray and uncaps them.

Noir catches Susannah's eye. "There's cause for celebration but how about we cover up first?"

As if cued, she and Susannah grip the tops of their ragged garments and hold them out and away from their torsos. "Badges of honor," Noir offers.

Grace rises and extracts a pair of shawls from a basket by the porch door. She tosses them to the women who wrap themselves in more decorous modesty.

"Last time I saw you two," she regards the pair accusingly, "you were at each other's throats. Now you're best buddies?"

Heather is curious. "Why am I thinking your *fight* was staged? And what's with those outfits?"

"It worked like a charm," Kirkallen repeats. "I credit Blackstone with the prurient details. The ripped dresses."

"The man's mind is usually not too far from the gutter," Susannah confirms. "No surprise he contributed that detail."

Blackstone remains mum. He wiggles his eyebrows.

Hardy hands a Balvenie to Kirkallen. "Just one, compadre." He resumes his place between the half-sisters and comments on the effervescent mood of the returnees, their angelic smiles. "Ladies," he says to Heather and Grace, "I'm not sure we want to hear precisely how our friends' recent activities Worked Like a Charm ..."

"... But we are about to find out," one of the daughters completes the father's thought.

Kirkallen sips his drink thoughtfully. Momentarily distracted, he holds it up. "The Navajo have a bunch of words for *whiskey*. One translates roughly to *Water of Darkness*. It was for me. Water of Darkness I mean. But," he tilts his glass toward Heather, Hardy and Noir, "not now. With the help of my friends I can now relish it in distinct moderation. This is the Water of Life." He savors another taste.

"Quit stalling," Heather scolds.

"Earth calling Kirkallen," Noir prompts.

Kirkallen launches into His Story. This one is surprisingly succinct. It's a real-life tale of deception and planned intrigue.

"Blackstone peels into the wash of a street lamp in a far corner of the marina lot. He brakes and skids and tires screech and Susannah and Noir are out in a flash, scattering the empty beer cans to set the scene and attract the guards, the downstate muscle. They're parked in their pickup by the heavy equipment. They're doing their shift, minding their own business when the girls take wild swings at each other and voice an impressive series of expletives and 'you bitches' and the promise of a cat fight appeals to the watchmen's baser instincts. They're seriously hoping to see some skin and cheer when Noir makes the first rip in Susannah's previously prepared outfit. The boys really let their dicks do the thinking and lose total regard for their assignment as Susannah tears at Noir's dress and the Siren of Seeing Even More Skin effectively seals the deal. The ladies have hooked the guards. They keep jousting and swearing.

"Then Blackstone and Carmody start working the men. They're slurring their words and sipping half empty Budweisers and they offer full cans to the guards to keep them from separating the ladies. They're using lines like *Let 'em solve their problems the old fashioned way, woman to woman* and *Don't break it up we're getting a good dose of skin* and *Here, have another Bud*. And that's where I come in …"

Kirkallen lifts his tool bag by the straps.

"It doesn't take long for a Brother who's handy with a wrench to take advantage of the action and slip away and loosen a few nuts and bolts and liberate some hoses and oil and fluids from the tractors."

"The best part is," Noir clarifies, "if the fluids stay underneath the tractors they may not even notice 'til Monday when they get ready to head to The Convent."

Heather claps in approval. "Maybe you didn't choose the most prudent course of action but it could give us more time when it comes to saving The Convent."

Grace puts a priestly spin on it. "Righteous people performing unrighteous deeds for a righteous cause."

Hardy grins approvingly. He can't remember when he's felt this happy but he needs to chastise his housemates. "You pulled this caper and didn't clue me in?"

"You were busy." Kirkallen nods toward Grace.

"There is that," Hardy admits. He places a hand on top of Grace's. "I have to know though. What about the other night? How the ..."

He checks his tongue, a fricative sound on its tip. "How on earth did you guys sneak away the other night to do that Invisible Stuff to the machinery that the mayor had on tape? I had no idea you were up to something."

A surprised expression crosses Noir's face. "The other night? Susannah and I were drinking at the brewery with the Sisters."

Kirkallen reminds his friend, "We crashed on the porch. Remember?"

"Blackstone and I were sleeping. Susannah was with the women," Carmody says.

Muskie's resting in her glider. She's gazing fixedly at an open space in the grouping of chairs. She thumps her tail on the wooden glider arm, producing a drumming sound.

"I have a feeling ..." Noir's voice drifts off. "Nah. No way," she scoffs.

"What?" Heather encourages.

"I have a feeling Muskie ... is seeing something, or somebody, we don't ... You think somebody's rocking her glider? Is that why she likes it so much? Why she only lies on half of it? Maybe she sees the ghosts of the House on the Hill? The spirits of Alexandra's clan?"

"I've been sensing weird vibes since I arrived," Blackstone cuts in. "Like someone I can't see is reaching out to me."

"Muskie?" Kirkallen asserts. "She must have some Navajo flowing in her veins. They believe in a Spirit World. In ghosts and witches and skin walkers. I think Muskie's seeing more than we do. Or can."

Later that night Hardy's haunted by a brief fleeting vision as he drifts off to sleep. It's Grace. She's wearing the Fried Egg Tee she wore the first time Hardy saw her.

Tomorrow he'll remember how and why it affected him the way it did.

❖

A GIFT FROM GOD

I didn't flinch on the porch last night when Micah Hardy put his hand over mine but I didn't expect it. He did it so easily and naturally. More a paternal reflex than a thought.

I didn't squeeze his in return. Nor did I pull away. It's perfect symbol for how I acted when Mama blurted Her News yesterday. You know I superficially held it together. I bet you expected more of an emotional reaction. I couldn't lose it then. If I did everyone would've gone to pieces. I needed to be strong for them and I knew I was tough enough to do it.

For the record? I was churning inside.

I still am. I hardly slept.

This morning I'm trying to frame my confusion. My thoughts are jumbled. I might jump around but I'm going to try to tell my story. I'll lead into it by sharing what I think I know.

I know I believe Mama. I know I believe Micah Hardy's my biological father. So the easiest place to begin is with a young Hannah Penner and a young Micah Hardy.

I know I'm glad they did what they did. Otherwise I wouldn't be here. I wouldn't be who and where I am.

I know I like Micah Hardy. That's a relief. I think he likes me too.

I know I don't know what to call him. Dad? Father? Micah? Hardy?

I know I shouldn't blame him for Not Knowing. But part of me wants to and I don't know why.

I know he's wearing his wedding ring. Fidelity counts for something.

I know he's confused. A lost soul.

I know he's too old to be trying to determine Who He Is.

I know my parents need time.

Mama? She's another story. She held out on me. I missed out on so much. So much of my father's life. So much of my mother and father's life together.

I bet you think I should be angry with her.

I'm not.

I know she was just trying to survive.

I know I wouldn't trade a second of my life for something different. I don't regret not having a father. I had three parents. I loved Grandma Miriam and Grandpa Isaac almost as much as I loved Mama. And they loved their daughter.

They didn't shame Mama when she came home with me in her belly. They opened their arms, literally and figuratively, and took Their Hannah in.

They agreed to call me *Grace*. A gift from God.

I enjoyed a stable home life and was mostly unaware I didn't have a father. After all I had Family. When I'd ask Mama about my father she'd respond with the same line.

He's not in our lives. There's no need to know.

Over time I stopped asking. I thought she might tell me eventually.

Grandpa acted the father to me. He taught me to fish and hunt and ride a horse and use his tools and drive a tractor. He ran his furniture business in a shop attached to the barn. He farmed the land on the side and took game—deer, pheasant, rabbits, catfish—when needed. I know how to use a filet knife. I've gutted more than one deer.

Grandma ran our home. She cooked, baked, cleaned, washed, sewed and tended the livestock. She harvested and canned her outsized vegetable garden. She turned fruit trees into pies and preserves, grapes into wine. She taught me how to behead a chicken and keep a garden.

As Mama took on work Grandma Miriam took on me. She literally took me in tow. I trailed her everywhere. We did chores at church. We traveled locally for service projects. Sometimes we ventured farther with the Mennonite Disaster Service. Once a year we did a Latin-themed mission trip. Nicaragua. Costa Rica. Ecuador. Peru. Venezuela. El Salvador.

I'm told our Mennonite community frowned on Mama's Delicate Condition. But they didn't fuss. They kept their opinions to themselves. They understood their duty and did it, offering help and love and support when necessary. Every time I walked or biked into town I knew watchful eyes watched me. On that subject I once heard Mama say *One more reason to name our child Grace.*

I liked school. I liked learning and reading and writing. I liked all the activities afterward. You have a lot of opportunities to do things at a small school—on the stage, in the band, on the field and in the gym.

I always loved music and church too. I loved the quiet and restful time in Sunday service when I could be alone with my thoughts.

I went to Sunday evening services. Wednesdays too.

I loved the singing. Everyone in the congregation knew music and notes. We sang beautiful hymns, often piecing out the parts.

I learned to trust in God and when the time came I affirmed my faith in Christ and took the baptizing.

It's Grandma Miriam who got me thinking about going away to school. She said I needed to see more of the world, find my place in it, find what I'm made of. She said it apologetically, ending with *Not like your mother and me …*

When I look back at it, her sentence trailed off with a sense of resignation. I think she wanted to see part of a life she never knew play forward in me. As much as I left home for college to find my own path I also left for Grandma Miriam. I wanted to do it for her too.

I happily accepted a scholarship and attended Goshen College. Immediately before I left I overheard Grandpa say to Grandma *It will be harder for a girl to Get in Trouble at a Mennonite school.* I've never told that to anyone.

I didn't learn much of the Big World in Goshen, Indiana. Nor did my range of vision widen more appreciably when, after graduation, I matriculated in a Virginia seminary. Then I did summer field work in North Philly, a neighborhood which at that time contributed dramatically to the town's description as The Poorest Big City in America. I found similar hovels in Camden and Baltimore and DC.

So much need, so much poverty. So little hope, so little time.

I didn't pursue ordination after completing my degree. My heart led me to mission work. I did a decade's-worth of it in Latin America, Harlem, Brooklyn and East LA. If you want I can speak with you in Spanish.

Though I found meaningful and rewarding employment I didn't know what I wanted to do. After experiencing life in those urban disaster zones I found a job helping people in literal ones. I moved to Lititz, Pennsylvania, and accepted a position with the Mennonite Disaster Service.

What about relationships? I like women. But not like that. Boys and men? I like them. But they are so ridiculous and most want One Thing. They're so darn predictable and vulnerable in their want.

I had quasi-serious relationships but nothing I ever wanted to put any work into in order for it to work out. There was one guy at the Relief Fund I could've married. He asked. He's a good man but for the life of me I couldn't pull the trigger.

Too much needed doing. And I didn't have enough time to do it.

That's when I moved to the Cities.

To be closer to Mama.

Once I left home that's where she went after Grandma and Grandpa died. To Minneapolis. If she wants she can tell you more about that.

I worked with Spanish-speaking immigrant families, documented or otherwise. I helped them find paths and make connections in a new country.

I discovered a Mennonite church to attend. They were searching for a pastor. It took more than a year but eventually Shalom Mennonite installed and licensed me. Mama proudly attended my ordination.

When I moved to Minnesota I wanted to show Mama how much I appreciated everything she gave up to make life easier for me. That's partly why I'm in Cedar Harbor now. I started coming to The House on the Hill when Mama and Abby first moved north. I love it here.

Of course I befriended Alexandra, and then Elizabeth. I discovered I could talk to these younger women in ways I couldn't, and don't, at home. We shared our hopes, mistakes, cares and spiritual concerns and basically laid our souls bare.

When Alexandra and Elizabeth disclosed the true nature of their relationship I replied with *You think I don't know? You think I'm not ready to ignore my church's policy if you want me to marry you?*

There. I've given you some background about me. It's easy to tell. And probably more than you want to know. But it is my way of telling you something about me when I don't know how to tell you how I'm feeling about discovering who my father is. And what I'm feeling about my mother and why she kept the news to herself as long as she did. Believe me, I'd share if I knew how to tell it.

I have a feeling I won't truly understand what I'm feeling for a long time. As long as I understand that, I can manage. I know my friends will help me. I know I can pray about it.

I need to pray now. I'm about to talk with my father. I'm headed into town to have an early coffee with Micah Hardy.

SHE'S FLAT-CHESTED LIKE ME?

I'm flattered and more than a trifle anxious when Grace asks me to meet in town to get acquainted, away from the group at The House on the Hill. We take a table by a window in Big Lake Coffee & Beans at six-thirty Sunday morning.

Our view of the lake is magnificent. It's as calm as I am not. The water lies smooth and quiet as far as we can see. Voices are muted; it's immediately noticeable customers are talking and listening. There's not a cell or tablet in sight.

You guessed it. I begin by sticking my foot in my mouth when I tell Grace about how when I noticed the fried eggs on her tee shirt the first time I saw her it reminded me of something, somebody I couldn't quite place and how I know now what I saw was a picture of how her college age mother looked and Grace says *You mean she's flat-chested like me?* and I say *Yes* and then we blush beet red.

When she laughs it off with *I don't suppose the best way to get to know a girl is to tell her she looks like her flat-chested mother right out of the gate*, I grin sheepishly and ask if she wants a coffee or a latté and she asks for an Americano saying she needs a jolt because she didn't sleep much last night and she's delivering the message at The Convent chapel later today.

It gets better fast after that.

I think Grace likes me.

Or is trying her best to like me.

She asks permission to call me *Micah* and I tell her I'm comfortable with whatever she chooses as long as she talks to me.

There you have it. It's a simple as that.

When I query her about the wedding and the possibility of losing licensure she shrugs. She's not concerned. She wishes her church would take a more moderate stance and recognize gays as fully human with fully human rights but she knows all denominations are arguing among themselves about that. She suspects her conference committee will want to review her credentials.

"They could suspend my license and even revoke it. It's more likely they'll put a note in my file indicating I am *at variance* with church polity by conducting the wedding. They'll keep their eye on me and I'm betting our congregation writes a letter supporting my actions. We have a pretty Lefty group."

She finishes with, "I did what I thought was right. I can live with the result."

What she says and how she says it makes my heart soar. I say her mother did a great job rearing her if that's how she's looking at it.

"Grandma Miriam and Grandpa Isaac too." Then she uses a wistful tone. "You would have liked them."

We retreat from that thought by sipping our drinks.

Of course I have to ask. This is the New Me.

Is Grace okay with finding out about me? Is she okay with her mother?

"You mean other than almost wetting myself with surprise? I had no idea. Once it sank in I mostly felt a sense of relief. Especially since you seem like a decent guy.

"I stopped worrying about your identity. I thought it would come out in due time. I felt no need to press. There's a piece of Mama, deep inside, I'll never know, let alone understand. She keeps this quiet center, a tough core like a resin-sealed jack pine seed which doesn't grow until it's heat-released by a forest fire. She finds comfort there. I think she takes comfort also in her sheer stubbornness. She is one tough lady."

Don't I know it?

I don't say that. I ask another awkward question instead. If she ever pressed her mother to find someone else.

"Why she never expressed attraction to any other man I'll never know. Probably because the pickings were slim in our small corner of the world. There was a widowed farmer. She worked for him when I was little. She mucked barns and baled hay and cooked his meals. Grandma Miriam told me once he offered marriage but I know Mama wanted more. I'm glad she went out and found it …"

When she lets the sentence trail off I sense we're at the end of talking about her mother. Things seem to be going okay. I ask if there's someone special in her life.

"I like men but I've never found The One. I'm too picky."

I can almost hear the gears grinding in her mind. Like she's considering saying more but doesn't. She changes the topic.

"How about we talk about you? Maybe you and Abby in particular? Now I know I'm your daughter and Abby is my kind of stepmother I have a right to an opinion, don't you think?"

I don't disagree and give her the space she wants and needs.

"You two are too old to act so childishly. You need to get your acts together and figure yourselves out. You owe it to yourselves. You owe it to us."

I say *I'll take that under advisement.* I admit it would be for the best. With the time I have left on this earth it makes sense.

"That's an understatement."

She glances out at the lake and sips her Americano. I'm not sure where she's going to take this conversation but I keep my peace.

"I hope we can talk more about you and Abby later but now I've gotten what I wanted to say off my flat chest, I'm wondering if you're coming to chapel today. To hear me speak? I love my Up North Girlfriends. Every time I preach here I feel nervous because I want to do an extra special job. I'd like to have you there. I hope to do an extra special job for you too."

Fortunately I have the good sense not to tell her I think Sunday is the saddest day in the Christian week.

It is The Divisional Day. All those denominations, worshipping the same God in often radically different ways, many believing dramatically different things, believing they've got the Inside Track on the Real Truth …

I tell her *I'm flattered she asked.* I tell her *I wouldn't miss it for the world.*

That's the real truth.

THE DITHER OF THE LAST SEVERAL DAYS

The chapel is small. Intimate without feeling claustrophobic. There's too much light for that.

Clean and clear windows are open to the brisk Superior air. There's a coat of fresh white paint on the walls. A dozen naturally finished pine pews are invitingly arranged under a beamed and vaulted ceiling. The maple floor gleams with new wax. There's a lectern up front and a plain oak table serves as an altar.

"Not a speck of dust or dirt," Kirkallen whispers. "These Convent Ladies take real good care in here but I see Issues. Things need fixing. If I wasn't in the company of so many women I'd say this place needs a man's hand."

"You just said it, chauvinist," Noir comments drily. Muskie's lying serenely at her feet.

"Mmm … don't misunderstand," Kirkallen begins. "It's a phrase. I'm not criticizing the Sisters. I don't necessarily buy into what they believe and how we're about to worship but I respect them for believing. I'd never take that away from them. I figure they're tuned into a wave length my radio doesn't have—or I can't find. That they're much smarter than me and understand something on a much higher and deeper level. All I'm saying is they could use a handyman."

Hardy's seated between Kirkallen and Noir. Though churchgoing generally raises his hackles he feels a certain peace as the lovely, simply elegant service unfolds. Regardless of what he believes, or doesn't, the ambiance is sacred. The tone reverent.

There's also a Certain Magic the Sisters bring to the ecumenical event. They employ hymns and prayers and readings to acknowledge a mixture of creeds grounded fundamentally in the Holy Trinity. Two plainly dressed women, community spiritual leaders, preside.

There's not a man in sight.

On the altar that is.

Then there's Grace. The preacher standing at the podium.

Hardy loves how she looks. He loves her melodic voice, her convincing tone and frank gaze.

This is one confident and together woman. The last thing she needs is a father to mess up her life.

Then he realizes the truth.

Grace already has one. A spiritual father. Or mother. She sounds and acts so secure in Her Faith and Life Path.

Yesterday's wedding has influenced Grace's scripture choice. She's taking on the familiar *1 Corinthians* text on love.

"For now we see in a mirror dimly, but then face to face. Now I know in part; then I shall understand fully, even as I have been fully understood. So faith, hope, love abide, these three; but the greatest of these is love."

Hardy ponders the Grace's choice of biblical text as she expounds. He fights the urge to criticize his independent minded daughter about using one of Paul's letters.

Paul. The Apostle notorious for assigning women to subordinate silent roles.

Hardy focuses on more immediate issues. He thinks he's doing a great job of seeming to take the complicated set of circumstances he's encountered since arriving at The House on the Hill in stride.

Internally? He's overwhelmed.

He snorts involuntarily when he catches himself lapsing into a sort of unvoiced prayer requesting guidance and clearer vision with regard to Elizabeth, Alexandra, Abby, Hannah and Grace—and His

Own Life. He also wonders if this Christian God has any ideas or answers.

The precise reason he mistrusts prayer. Asking God's help with the Little Things when so many Big Issues confront our world. His mind wanders further afield to the absurdity of athletes praying for victory or thanking God for helping them hit home runs.

Muskie stirs from her post. She's more finely attuned to the spirit world than Hardy. She senses Hardy's confusion and inner turmoil. She rises on her haunches and places her chin on her friend's thigh. Noir leans into Hardy. She presses her leg next to his and rests her head against his shoulder. She's in tune too.

It's a comforting feeling and Hardy sighs deeply, letting the dither of the last several days escape as he breathes slowly and evenly. Peaceful.

He feels an odd sense that things are only just beginning.

ENLARGE THE TEMPLE

I can't believe I'm sitting in church.

It's been a long time. But the ground didn't shake when I entered.

I especially can't believe I'm in This Church. Listening to my daughter preach. The daughter I didn't know I fathered.

Until yesterday.

The Mennonite reverend.

You gotta admit I've seen a bunch of curve balls lately. And yeah I'm thrown off balance by them. Grace tops the list. Abby and Hannah are tied for second.

My Grace? Do I dare think that?

Our Grace? A heavy concept. Do I dare say that?

The astonishing thing is it's like Grace knows me, understands my confusion. It's like she's speaking to me. Her message has shifted gears. She's quoting a poet. W.S. Merwin.

"'If you find you no longer believe,'" and she pauses and stares at me. "'If you find you no longer believe, enlarge the temple.'"

Precisely.

Enlarge the temple.

She's hit the core of it. Or Merwin has.

I need to enlarge my temple.

I'm more than eager to make room for other creeds and other ways to believe but I've closed out the ones I love best. I need to make the same room for Grace's Way of Believing. For Abby's and Hannah's. I need to understand nobody's perfect. Nobody's got The Right Way to Believe. That's what I was trying to say about Sunday being the saddest day of the Christian week.

I'm thinking God's more imperfect than the rest of us. Another huge reason why the temple needs to be bigger.

It is true we've been disappointing God for thousands of years. What's truer is God's been disappointing humans for thousands of years, never quite delivering.

Look around. You don't have to look very far.

How many international hotspots can you name?

What about race relations in this country?

Or all the school shootings?

Consider the stability of any number of our world leaders, particularly those with access to nuclear weaponry.

It's enough to make anybody with a lick of sense to start praying.

Seriously.

My daughter is finishing her sermon.

"Think about opening your heart when it's the hard thing to do. Open your heart when it's the hard thing to do because," she takes a breath, "it is assuredly the right thing to do."

"Amen," someone says.

It might be me.

After a closing hymn and a brief prayer, Abby stands for an announcement.

"Speaking of the Right Thing to Do, we need you to do the right thing tomorrow morning—or this could be the last service we conduct in this building. Please join us bright and early at the entrance to The Convent drive. It's time to take a stand against development. Stand for The Convent. Stand against DSG."

"Amen," someone says.

This time it's not me.

But I think it.

SEVEN

A FLIGHT OF ANGELS

THE RAIN POUNDS AND THE SKY DARKENS

The lake is placid in the early light, a sheet of dark slate snoozing under a low ceiling thick with gray-graphite cloud. *Storms's brewing*, Kirkallen thinks while he completes his stretching on the grass outside his cottage.

By six, Superior behaves as one large entity. The water's undulating from shore to horizon with the promise of weather when The House on the Hill Contingent crams into a convoy of vehicles and heads forth to battle.

They motor purposefully through town to The Convent entrance where a loyal group of citizens is congregated. Everyone's wearing waterproofs in anticipation of the approaching disturbance. Their parkas ripple and snap in the sharpening breeze.

Marion arrived predictably early. She's set out a table on which she's placed an air void of hot coffee alongside two tubes of compostable cups. A stack of placards leans against a table leg. She's waiting expectantly when Hannah and Abby pull into the drive. She motions them ahead. The lead protestors park their truck sideways across the drive.

They emerge and begin organizing. Hannah gives marching orders to the townspeople while Abby confers with the Sisters and various Significant Women Protesters—including Alexandra, Elizabeth, Grace,

Heather and her daughters, Marion, Noir, Susannah and Violet. There are audible gasps as the ladies confer and absorb instruction.

"It'll be easier than you think," Susannah states calmly.

Then she says something remarkable. "The older you get the more invisible you become to men. We're freer because of it. Our lives are no longer defined by our bodies. Our lives are written on our faces."

The business of protest proceeds. Hannah huddles briefly with The Lads and joins the Significants.

Hardy and Kirkallen take Milwaukee aside. Will he manage the background guys? When he hears it's what Abby and Hannah want, he puffs with pride and marshals his charges.

Women know how to play to a man's ego. A timeworn practice.

Milwaukee arranges his regiment in a two deep line across the entrance, extending it onto the grass to each side of the macadam, effectively restricting access to motorized vehicles.

When a beat-up Dodge Ram turns into the drive, Milwaukee assumes sentry duty. The driver brakes and the brewer places his hands flat on the hood. He smiles when the high school football coach pops his head out the window.

"Ed? What are you doing?"

"Come to support The Cause." He jerks a thumb toward the pickup bed. "I brought the sideline capes like Abby asked."

"Capes?"

"Capes," he repeats simply. "That's all I know."

"Abby asked for them?"

"Yes."

"That's all I need to know." Milwaukee clears a path and lets the truck pass.

There's the sound of rumbling engines. Oversized transport vehicles pulling wrecking machines. The yellow line is led by Mayor Karvonen's new truck, the sheriff's black-and-white and the iron gray SUVs. They brake to a stop.

The mayor and his sidekick, developer-banker David Shire, emerge from the Silverado to a chorus of catcalls from placard-holding citizens. Sheriff Ralph Gustafson joins the pair. They deliberately approach

Milwaukee and the obstructing men and halt about ten feet away. There is a pregnant pause which Muskie punctuates with a low-throated growl. She's standing next to Hardy. He holds a *Save The Convent* poster.

The mayor shuffles awkwardly toward Milwaukee, his suit ill-fitting as if purchased secondhand. He apologizes. "Sorry we're late. We ... ah ... had to replace some vehicle fluids. Some nuts and brake lines and hoses got loosened over the weekend. Must've been one of those ghosts that dog sees."

Muskie growls and the hair stands up on her spine.

"Easy girl," Hardy mutters.

Muskie sits.

The mayor gropes for an inside jacket pocket. "I've brought some legal documents." He unfolds them, half offering the papers to the group, half shielding himself from the mutt. "I've asked the sheriff along to keep everything on the up-and-up."

"And I'm here to see the law upheld. To see we get our due," Shire intones. He sports a tailored European suit and the impatient facial expression of a Privileged White Man who expects to get his way. His hands are clean, his nails are manicured. His soul is filthy.

Kirkallen leans into Hardy and whispers, "Dude's suit is worth more than my entire wardrobe. Even if you award full value to the two Harris Tweed sports coats I picked up for seven bucks apiece at the Goodwill."

"I'm obliged to enforce the law and keep the peace," Gustafson cautions. "I don't like it. I'd rather see The Convent stay as is but the law's the law. Justice must be served."

Hardy flashes on how he used to perform distasteful functions in behalf of his employer. He breathes a sigh of relief. He's pleased to be free of Gayle Harte's directives and is surprised to hear his voice rise above the wind.

"Justice is not just when it's not right."

There is general applause.

Abby and Hannah appear from behind the line of citizens. They emerge silently, as if out of the cornfield onto Shoeless Joe's Field of Dreams. They're cloaked in scarlet shin length football parkas, the fronts snapped closed.

Hannah underscores her Mennonite heritage. "We're gathered peacefully as you can see."

"But you may have to move us," Abby states firmly. "You might not like the process. Could prove awkward for your boys."

"Could be very awkward," Hannah emphasizes her friend's point.

The scene is silent save the sounds of weather and water. Individual raindrops splash on the road surface and vehicle hoods.

Abby and Hannah exchange anxious glances. *Ready? We can do this.* Each unsnaps several parka closures.

Backs to the protestors they lower their capes and hold them over the tops of their breasts. The ladies have discarded their blouses and brassieres.

Karvonen, Shire and Gustafson step back as if they've peed on an electric fence. Their mouths drop open.

"Your boys might not like removing us if we remove these." Abby slides her cape down further to accentuate her intent.

The rain intensifies as the Significants line up behind their co-leaders. They're wearing Cedar County High football capes.

"You'll have to remove us too," Grace announces snapping open her top button. "Want to see more? Boys usually do."

Milwaukee reappears in the frame. "We men won't stand aside if you move them."

He nods skyward and then out to the highway. "You also might get wet in the process. Not to mention the traffic jam you've created. You haven't noticed the sky? You haven't noticed your machinery's blocking the highway? Sheriff? You got a man to direct traffic?"

As if cued, the heavens open and the deluge commences, forcing the enforcing trio to retreat to Karvonen's crew cab where they confer.

The rain pounds and the sky darkens.

Oblivious to the downpour, the expectant protestors hold their breath. Kirkallen busies himself by filling empty cups with steaming coffee.

The sheriff emerges and approaches the defiant women. Their hair is soaked, plastered to their heads. Water streams off their bare shoulders.

"I asked Karvonen and Shire to stand down today. They've agreed. The weather's nasty. I didn't plan for the traffic. I also didn't think I'd have to deal with the likes of half-naked ladies."

He takes a breath before continuing. "You're so darn audacious. You make me proud. Not giving up without a fuss. Good for you. Good for Cedar Harbor. We don't need no condos. But I'm an officer of the law. I have my job to do. I can delay the eviction but not for long. I respect what you're doing but I don't want to peek under those parkas."

He bends into a gallant bow. "Ladies, we'll bid you good day but we're coming back tomorrow."

"We'll be here."

Everyone says it.

A COUPLE OF IDEAS I'D LIKE TO RUN BY YOU

There is a collective cheer as the trucks depart. Abby and Hannah clamber into the pickup bed to address the group.

Hannah begins in softening rain. "Thank you for coming out this morning. Our Sisters are grateful. We are grateful." She pokes Abby in the ribs. "We planned on winning today though we did gamble on the element of surprise ..."

The group laughs as she snaps the top button of her parka authoritatively closed.

"... and we did get help from the weather. I don't know about you but I'm calling it Divine Intervention."

"Amen," a chorus from the crowd agrees.

Abby takes up the cause. "This was our opening skirmish. We need you here tomorrow morning. And to encourage you to do so we're inviting you inside now. Our Sisters have prepared some nourishment for you." She motions to Sister Marion. "Marion? Will you tell us about it?"

Kirkallen cups his hands to offer a boost. Hardy joins him and provides a willing shoulder. Together they help the dark-skinned woman into the back of the truck.

"I can't thank you enough for coming." Marion's face is glowing. "Please join us in our dining room. We've got towels and dry clothes for those who need them. After Pastor Grace blesses the food we'll put out, you're welcome to share a meal and fellowship. It's our small way of thanking you for today."

"It's also our way of saying *Come back tomorrow*," Abby interjects.

When the applause subsides Marion closes with, "Let's go inside and get out of this Blessed Rain."

There is genuine goodwill and camaraderie as the buffet event unfolds. It is an opportunity for the locals to see The Convent and chat with the Sisters.

Hannah and Abby are standing quietly to one side of the assembly. They're enjoying the moment but understand the bigger challenge lies ahead. "This may be our only victory," Hannah muses.

Abby is about to reply but the pair is distracted by an approaching stranger. He holds a white towel and mops his hair which he pulls into a scraggly damp pony tail.

He stops in front of them and bows slightly. He is short and carries the body of someone familiar with a weight room. His earnest brown eyes are set into an equally earnest face.

"Ladies? We haven't met but I feel I know you. I've streamed your WCED broadcasts. I listen at my office desk in the Cities. They say you're 'liberal but even minded thinkers,' don't they?"

"Sir?" Hannah queries.

"I'm a friend. Or I hope you see me as one. I'm a lawyer. I'm in town doing some *pro bono* work for the Birchwood School. I think you know it?"

"Birchwood does good work. I hear they're struggling financially. I'm pleased you're helping." Abby steps toward the man and extends her hand. "You seem to know us. We'd like to know you."

The man accepts Abby's hand. "Scott Davidson. Esquire."

"How can we can help you?"

"On the contrary. I'm thinking I might be of assistance to you. I'm also thinking you may be able to help the school. Do you have a private place where we can chat? I have a couple of ideas I'd like to run by you."

THE BOYS CAN'T SIGN FAST ENOUGH

I figured I'd had my quota of Surprises for the Year with the wedding and the recent epiphanies. But this takes the cake. I've never seen anything like it.

Except maybe at a strip club.

No. Not even there.

You ever see a line of twenty or so mostly older women with their tops off? You ever see that same group blocking entry to a convent driveway?

Trust me. I don't think you want to.

Especially when the chill off the lake has tightened every nipple. Even more so when one of the women is your wife, another is a long-ago lover, three are your daughters, another is your daughter-in-law, one's a roommate you consider a daughter and others are newfound friends.

Heather's girls, Olivia and Amelia, stepped forward too. Heather had the good sense to keep them in sports bras.

And then there's Kyle. My son-in-law-the-photographer is capturing images for posterity.

As much as I want to look away, I can't. I have to see how this plays out. I'll try to scrub my memory clean later.

What I can't scrub from my mind is the clarity of scene. The drama.

Yesterday's rain has cleared. The sky's bright blue. A faint breeze wafts off the lake. The surface is undisturbed and studded with diamonds. It's sleeping, breathing gently, barely audible, respecting the moment. Wavelets sigh quietly against primordial rock.

There's bird song. A chorus of mating and nesting migrants—warblers, vireos, waxwings and thrushes. They're celebrating the protest.

God's music.

The assembled group is as hushed as the birds are jubilant. No one has witnessed this kind of spectacle.

Topless Sisters? My word.

It's Scott's idea to jolt the men out of their comfort zones. He says all the women should follow through with yesterday's threat. They should disrobe.

He admits our ploy is outrageous and startling.

That's the point.

He says the men'll get fidgety and downright nervous and want to disappear if we give them an excuse to be gone. He says he'll give them that excuse. Make them feel they've won. When in actuality they'll be signing something they'd never agree to.

So there are my Abby and Hannah. They're standing up to Shire and Karvonen and Gustafson. Square shouldered and bold as brass. Their feet planted like roots. The ladies' eyes are clear, their jaws set. They've put their trust in their Lord.

Some in shock value too.

The mayor and the developer are a mismatched pair. A cultivated Armani-clad businessman with a private school education and an Ivy League degree. A bumpkin with a state college diploma and a blue collar upbringing.

A man the System Serves.

A man who Used the System to gain advantage.

The men are patently unnerved. All they want is to be somewhere else. Anywhere.

Hannah hands over a *Cease and Desist* document. Three densely worded pages printed in small type.

She apologizes. She says she never thought the Lord wouldn't give them the help they needed. They didn't prepare to vacate as they should.

"We will step aside," she allows, "but we're demonstrating here because we want to make you as uncomfortable as possible before we do. We want you to remember who we are. What we stand for."

She asks for three days. Time to pack and clear out and make ready for demolition.

"It's all in the document. You sign. We sign. We agree not to block your vehicles."

She points to the agreement and cautions, "Read it first. Check the fine print."

I watch as Abby raises her hand and the line of women strides forward in concert. They circle Karvonen and Shire. Gustafson holds up his hands and backs off.

More breasts than they've ever seen at once. The boys can't sign fast enough. "We'll see you Friday."

They bid *adieu* and motor away.

WOMEN OF ALL STRIPES

The ladies can't believe they did that. Can't believe they took off their shirts.

Women of all stripes.

Women of faith.

Women of conscience, doing what they think is right, acting for the Common Good.

They're giddy. With shock. With victory. They're uncorking green bottles of sparkling white wine. A tad early since it's barely coffee break.

The Lord works in mysterious ways.

What did Karvonen and Shire sign?

They think they hold an agreement allowing them to raze The Convent and erect condominiums. They do, but that's open to interpretation.

Let's back up.

Scott says Birchwood needs temporary classroom space while they do urgent rehab work on their auxiliary building. He knows The Convent has room.

Wouldn't it be refreshing to liven up The Convent atmosphere by hosting a couple of elementary school classes for a summer school term?

Add a pinch of youthful exuberance to life at the staid Convent? Maybe they form a choir? How about blending the kids' cherubic voices with more mature ones and singing together in the chapel?

In return Scott believes he's found a glitch in the legal process. He wants to do some research. That's why *Cease and Desist* gives him until Friday.

The Give Us Three Days Line is a ploy. It buys time but not enough to sound unreasonable.

Scott drove to the county court house to check some real estate records. Then he nosed through a sheaf of historic family documents Alexandra found when she first arrived in Cedar Harbor.

An older Birchwood teacher, a longtime resident, told Scott she remembered a Wives Tale that got plenty of airplay.

Supposedly Robert Kerr included a rider in the contract he signed with the Original Sisters. Scott thinks the stipulation essentially amounts to a Land Trust that restricts additional property development. If he can find the contract he thinks he can stop the project in its tracks.

No development? No condos.

Scott's also positive his digging can expose the trumped-up code violations that doomed The Convent to begin with. He says he can create a Win-Win Situation.

Think about it. What's a piece of land without a project worth to a developer?

It's a tax liability.

The Town Council has not yet expended the funds from Shire's initial property purchase. The council will fold to public pressure and refund his cash. The developer can claim a loss on the rest and write off the amount he invested in R&D and planning.

He'll happily—well, not happily—leave town.

And the Sisters will happily—very happily—reclaim their property.

What's not to like?

Two things.

First. It's likely the mayor forfeits his new pickup. Not many will be unhappy about that. But the mayor sure will.

Then there's item 8.1 in *Cease and Desist* that will frost Shire's Gorgonzolas.

Section 8 will rattle. He'll be required to express regret for inconveniencing the Sisters and town residents for the upheaval he precipitated. He'll declare publicly he wishes to make amends.

Item .1 will bite.

In this section Shire indicates his willingness to build a community pool and to provide five years of upkeep and maintenance.

Want to make a wager? Shire fires his lawyer.

It's evening and the sun has set and I'm sitting in a lawn chair outside our cabins with Olivia and Amelia. My granddaughters have beamed all day after joining the Bold Women and doing their own G-rated expression of protest.

"I'm so proud of our mom and Grandma and Aunt Hannah and all of them. So proud I could burst," Amelia says.

I tell them I'm proud too. That they should note How Strong Women Behave. What they can do when they pull together.

With that Olivia yawns and stretches. "Grandpa, we don't need a lecture. We know strong women when we see them." She rises, "I need to sleep. I've had a *too-big day.*"

Too-big day. Heather used to say that as a little girl when she felt over stimulated.

THEY DIDN'T ACTUALLY GET A FAIR CHANCE

If you've read this far don't blame me. I'm only telling the story, though I admit I'm confused. I'm talking and sharing so much I'm struggling to discern if I'm talking to you or the Narrator is. This is me now.

It's up to you to decide which one that is.

But if you have read this far I bet you're pleased it appears Shire and Karvonen are about to get their comeuppance.

Like me you're rooting for the Good Guys over the Bad Guys.

For Right routing Wrong.

For Good Works scoring over Greed.

For the Environment drubbing Development.

My Holy Women, devout believers and do-gooders, are feeling pretty good too.

Abby and Hannah. Libby and Alexandra. Heather and her girls. Noir. Grace. Susannah and Violet and Marion. And of course the handful of convent residents. The Sisters.

I'm happy for them, delighted in fact. But as I consider the women in my life, they befuddle me.

Libby because, other than my sheer asininity, I never understood what closed my mind and door to her for so long. I understand even less why she let me open it again. For that I am grateful. I have to remember to call her *Elizabeth*.

Grace because she's Grace. A virtual unknown. A forty-something minister. And a daughter I didn't know until two days ago.

Then there's Heather. The steadfastly loyal daughter who's stuck by me. The one who fishes with me. I can't for the life of me figure out what I did to deserve her kindness and forbearance and love.

Speaking of steadfast, how can Noir live with two old farts like me and Kirkallen? I know we puzzle her but she confounds us with her continuing love and cooking. And movie quotes. We love her. I know she's said she loves us. Has one of us admitted that out loud to her? We both should.

Those folks are the Bit Players in this saga. The Primary Two are a true puzzle.

Abigael Delaney. My tough wife who is by all appearances done with me, does not need me, let alone want me. But she is treating me gently, permitting the waters to flow quietly. She's being downright gracious. Especially when you consider I have a daughter by her best friend.

Hannah Penner? The lovely Hannah who drifted out of my consciousness and marched back into my life? Who is she? I dimly remember the girl I was crazy about. This new woman is a mystery. And a storm trooper.

What I chiefly know about this duo is how devout they are. How devoted they are to Jesus. How focused they are on their social causes and spiritual practices.

They are everything I am not.

These women who confuse me? They are tougher than I. Maybe because they've had to be to survive in a Man's World.

Why is it, then, I feel slightly uncomfortable about their method? I'm thinking they're cheating.

It is cheating when you Bend the Rules or Shade the Truth, right?

How is it these holy and noble women are so happy to gain an extra few days by deceiving those hapless men, distracting the hell out of them at a lakeside standoff with an up-close display of bared flesh?

If I were those guys and all those breasts staring at me? I'd sign on the dotted line and get my ass gone too.

Trouble is, they didn't actually get a fair chance to know what they were signing. When I express this privately to Noir she provides a lightning-quick rationale from *North by Northwest* where Cary Grant defines Truth in Advertising.

Something about there's never a lie, merely "expedient exaggeration."

I'll have to think about that.

But people do cheat in the Bible. Take Jacob, a respected Judeo-Christian patriarch. Didn't he refuse to give his hungry brother a bowl of soup until Esau agreed to relinquish his birthright? Didn't he lie to his father to steal his older brother's inheritance? And yet … God blessed this dishonorable liar and cheater. What's with that?

But don't misinterpret my disorientation. My wonderings are abstract, part of my philosophical inquiry as I try to figure Christianity in my juvenile fashion. The closer I consider it the crazier it seems. I need to remember to enlarge my temple.

Be assured that in the real world I'm stoked the ladies have a good chance of getting their Convent back.

I can't wait to swim in that new pool.

In the meantime Scott is completing his research. As confused as I am I know for certain I'm not going home. If I did I'd be leaving

Kirkallen and Noir and Muskie behind. They're committed to seeing this Convent Thing through. As are Heather and the girls.

Kyle's gotta go. There's work to do. Blackstone's leaving too. He's bound for France to play a few gigs.

Alexandra and Elizabeth are happy Susannah and Carmody are staying. We'll get them home somehow.

I think that about tells you where things stand so I'll walk over to the porch. Kirkallen's out there. I bet he's rolling a thin one.

AN EVEN MORE ASTONISHING TURN OF EVENTS

As the crowd enters Cedar County Courthouse the wind shifts to the southwest under a moderate blue sky, the undulating lake a deeper blue below it. The steady breeze kicks the water into corrugation. It laps in persistent intervals against the ancient harbor rock. Away from shore white caps are frothing.

The Cedar Harbor Town Council convenes on short notice to hear and consider Scott Davidson's presentation and Shire's defense. The tiny room is packed with interested onlookers. To a person they're partisan to The Convent Cause.

Due to her participation in the events precipitating the session, alderwoman Abigael Delaney recuses herself. She sits with her friends at the rear of the hall.

Muskie has nosed in. She focuses on a vacant corner of the room. Like she's seeing something no one else does. Or can.

For a lawyer, Scott gives the appearance of a sincere and honest man. Perhaps he is. We know he likes a good IPA. We've philosophized over a couple in Milwaukee and Violet's pub. A good place to start.

The sturdy counselor speaks confidently. He knows what he's doing. And when he lets his readers drop from his eyes to hang from a retainer cord around his neck we discover he's about to make a long-winded point using big words.

He fashions a genuinely believable case, citing precedent and noting sections of the zoning code that contradict the Council's decision regarding The Convent's alleged violations. Then he produces an aged parchment document.

It closes the deal.

He presents Kerr's original contract with the Sisters. It contains a paragraph that amounts to a Restrictive Covenant, effectively a land trust. It prohibits large-scale development on the property and it's signed by Robert Kerr, his wife and convent representative, Sister Rose Patrice. The document also bears an official Cedar County seal of acceptance and filing.

Shire's lawyer can mount no reasonable defense.

In the end the deliberative body, clearly sensing the mood of the citizenry and fixing its eyes on the prospect of a donated public pool, votes unanimously to void the project.

Shire concedes graciously. In return he's permitted to name the pool as he chooses. Within reason.

"He's giving in too easily. He must have found a convenient financial loophole," Hardy ventures.

"You mean like allowing him to write this whole thing off?" Kirkallen asks.

"Who cares?" Noir responds. "What matters is we got The Convent back."

"We?" Hardy questions, edging an elbow into his friend's rib cage. "Since when did you become a Holy Roller? You joining up? Moving in?"

"We need to make more space in this world for people to do good work." The serious young woman crinkles her eyes in thought. She paraphrases Sydney Greenstreet in *The Maltese Falcon*.

"They're characters, those ladies are. There's never any telling what they'll do next, except it's bound to be something astonishing."

What is equally astonishing is Mayor Karvonen unexpectedly bows out.

He tenders his resignation.

He's leaving town. He'll summer at his lake cabin. It's a guess, but reasonable to assume, he'll be leaving without his new truck.

In an even more astonishing turn of events the Council moves unanimously to appoint Abigael Delaney acting mayor of Cedar Harbor.

The conclave closes and the crowd gathers in celebration on the courthouse plaza overlooking the lake. On the road below a line of yellow heavy equipment, led by the gray SUVs, threads out of town in the direction of the Twin Cities.

"Superior Brewing's opening early," Milwaukee announces. "I'm tapping a keg and firing up the charcoal. Y'all come over in a few and bring some meat to burn. The suds are on us."

Kirkallen and Noir and Hardy prepare to head up the hill before going to Milwaukee's but they can't find Muskie.

She's remained in the council chambers, lying peacefully in the corner, content in the company of a Kerr ghost or two.

"I think maybe the Kerrs can rest easy." Noir sounds like she believes in what Muskie's seeing.

I know I do.

BURN A LITTLE SAGE

"When."

It's a word Noir once told me I can't pronounce.

She linked it to an obscure Bogart movie, *Isle of Fury*. There's a scene where a weathered South Sea Island doctor is offered a drink and instructed to say the word when his glass is sufficiently full. The Caucasian suit clad doc is a rummy. He pulls on his pipe and mutters wistfully, "That's a word I can't pronounce."

I used to be that guy when it came to booze. But I can say *when* now. Thanks to Noir and Hardy and Heather and a host of others.

It takes a village and I am profoundly grateful.

This is Kirkallen. Aside from describing the events in the harbor parking lot they've kept me quiet thus far. They say I talk too much, that my stories take elaborate detours. Hardy and Noir and the Narrator protest that my voice will add a hundred pages to the novel.

So what?

What good story doesn't take a winding path and throw in subplots? For what it's worth this tale is wandering all over the map without my input. It's left to me to simplify matters. Or at least try.

I would've stayed if they'd tried to build that golf course at The Convent. I'd've peed in every golf hole they set into their putting greens. Besides the affront of tearing up the land, they'd be wasting good Superior water to keep a lawn growing where it makes no sense for one to exist. Whatever else you've been reading about Hardy's Questions with regard to religion and God, it's an affront to God to build that golf course.

I have a purpose in breaking in here. Hardy needs me. All he's got in Saint Paul is a house.

He's found Family in Cedar Harbor.

So stick with me. I'm going to lay some basic Navajo on you. I'll do my best to keep on track.

Before I begin I have to do is apologize to the *Dineh* in case I'm getting their story, or thinking, wrong. I don't mean to. I'm a simple Brother trying to put my life together. The Navajo Way is helping me out big time. I'm grateful for that.

Maybe I can use it to help others too.

I'll play the Family Card first.

Maintaining positive familial connections is essential to anyone's walk with beauty. When one Navajo introduces himself to a tribe member, the first thing he does is share his family lineage—who he's Born To on his mother's side, who he's Born For on his father's side. It's important to know your clan.

There is no greater compliment to a Navajo than to say he takes care of his relatives.

And no greater insult than to criticize him by saying he behaves like he has none.

Here's the ploy.

Hardy needs to stay in Cedar Harbor.

Where his Family is.

Starting with his daughter. The one who married Alexandra and lives at The House on the Hill. The one he didn't talk to for several years. Elizabeth. He needs to make up for lost time.

What else is he doing except trout fishing with me?

Then my man has to pull his head out from his hindquarters and solve the Abby Equation. They *need* to Get Right on that score. As tough as they act and as cool as they think they are at handling their separation they're broken people.

They're the only ones who can't see it.

That's how broken they are.

They need to figure out Who They Are When They Are Together. They need to make room for each other. To enlarge their temples. Trust me, they want to but they don't know how.

If they don't talk it out they'll never be whole. If they don't get their acts together soon, Yours Truly will be sitting down with them.

I know they don't want that.

Then there's Hannah. The Old Girlfriend.

The Old Girlfriend who had her guy's baby and didn't tell him.

This is thorny.

Don't get me wrong. I know this story's a fairy tale but we're not taking it as far as to include a new romance—other than Libby's and Alexandra's.

We're certainly not getting into any three sided relationships.

Besides, and don't tell Hardy I'm tattling here, he'd kill me. Romantically speaking, and referring obliquely to The Bard's *Antony and Cleopatra*, "The soldier's pole is fall'n."

You get my drift?

Old Flame or not, Hardy's got to settle with Hannah. Even though their kid is full grown, they have a chance to be Family and need to figure out how they'll make that work in a way that works for all of them. That includes Abby too.

I'm also thinking Hannah needs healing.

No. I know Hannah needs healing.

Keeping the Grace-Hardy Connection secret for so long?

Withholding that information from her daughter and the daughter's father?

Whoa.

She needs to right that wrong.

This is basic *Dineh*. If you harm a person or a family group you sit down with them and right the wrong. That's what Hannah needs to do.

Part of her heart must be heavy. Part of her soul must be frostbitten.

Maybe that's why she's so seriously into social justice causes. She's spent her whole life trying to make things right for others probably in part to avoid making things right with her own self.

No apology required here. There's no need for recrimination. Hannah doesn't need punishment.

She needs curing.

To be restored to beauty. It's the Navajo Way.

I haven't forgotten Grace. The beautifully simple, simply beautiful middle aged pastor who's put her ministerial license on the line and recently learned who her father is.

She seems to be taking it all in stride but I'm guessing there's a heavy Inner Turmoil she's not sharing. And living on her own in the Cities with no one to talk to? I'm thinking that's not such a good thing.

I think I've got the cure for this one. Noir said something about it earlier but it's up to me to make it happen.

Hardy and Noir and I have an extra bedroom in Saint Paul. Say Grace moves in and, short-term, Hardy and I vacate to give the girls space? I bet pretty soon Grace and Noir and Heather and her girls are thick as thieves. Like sisters.

They know they can drive north too. They know where to find us. They know where their family is.

So we need a bunch of healing here—and Hardy and Hannah and Abby and Elizabeth and Grace probably represent the tip of the iceberg. What I'm wishing is I wish I knew how to conduct a Healing Ceremony.

I don't want to try to approximate one. I wouldn't want to be disrespectful to the Navajo.

What I can do is talk with and listen to my friends. We could burn a little sage, roll a thin one and consider our needs and feelings. I simply need to stay tuned in and seize the moment when the opportunity presents itself.

You know I have a horse in this race too.

Two horses really.

First? I've taken an interest in one of the Sisters at the Convent. I think Marion likes me. That's interesting since I like her. She's not a religious Sister. She's an ethnic one, if you get my drift. Who knows how that could play out?

I also don't want to leave Cedar Harbor. I don't want to leave The House on the Hill.

Especially if it means returning to the Cities.

Who in his right mind would want to return to neatly plotted streets, planned greenery, traffic, congestion, noise and nearby neighbors? Speaking of which? With our neighbor-witch living next to us in Saint Paul? It's gotten so a body can't even take a decent whiz in his own back yard.

This is the one piece of the puzzle I know I've put in place.

We're not going back.

I'll tell you how I'll work that in a bit. Or somebody will. Now I need to bike down the hill and catch the ex-mayor before he heads to his lake place. He'll be needing to do something with his new truck and I have an idea.

INTERESTED IN HEARING US OUT?

Hardy's Suburban is seventeen years old. Its roof is pocked with rust. The windshield's cracked. The air conditioner gave up the ghost years ago. The remote door opener never worked properly. The right rear panel is dented and the bumper cap is missing. The seal on the passenger side rear door window is missing; the gap is sealed with Frog

Tape. The truck's so dated Chevy stopped making the replacement piece.

It's best not to ask Kirkallen about the dent. He'd lament encountering unseen black ice on a curve in a freeway underpass in fifteen-below weather.

He'd also say Hardy needs a new vehicle and Hardy'd counter by bragging about keeping the truck in good running order and never making monthly payments on it to begin with. He occasionally editorializes about cheap insurance and registration fees.

As supper scents waft out of the kitchen Hardy and Noir are lounging on the porch at The House on Hill. They lift their glasses of Milwaukee's pale ale at Kirkallen's approach. Muskie has abandoned her post on the glider. She lies contentedly at their feet and thumps her tail in greeting.

The first thing they notice is Kirkallen is driving. This is odd since he doesn't own a car. It's even odder he's driving the mayor's Silverado.

The trim African-American man flashes a wide smile as he exits the vehicle. "Mayor had to give his truck back to the developer."

Kirkallen halts his explanation. He considers his word choice while he walks toward the porch.

"Shire? The developer guy? His shorts were bundled tight with the idea of having a pickup in Cedar Harbor and no driver to take it home. He said they used the truck around the dealership for chores and long distance deliveries. Offering it to the mayor at a huge reduction ... how exactly did he put it? *Giving it to that asshole mayor sealed the development deal.*

"It turns out the truck's pretty much brand new. He actually asked if I wanted to deal. He gave me some legalese about having to write this whole condo fiasco off and seeing that truck on his lot would piss him off because it would remind him of ... I'll use his words again, *that shit-for-brains mayor and my shit-for-brains business scheme.*"

"You mean you bought it?" Hardy asks incredulously. He and Noir stand in unison.

"*We* bought it," Kirkallen corrects. "For a song. But first I pretended not to want it and he reduced the price."

"Who's *we?*"

"You and me, partner." Kirkallen raises the title to display it. "All you have to do is sign on the dotted line."

Hardy visibly relaxes after Kirkallen mentions the outrageously reasonable price tag.

"I guess we have a new truck."

"Hmmphh. Highway robbery." Noir sips thoughtfully at her ale, places it deliberately on the railing, wraps her arm around Hardy's waist and pulls the tall awkward man to her side. "You've always wanted a pickup. You can cross that off your Bucket List. So what's next? What else do you want?"

"A good question," Hardy concedes.

"Whatever you want it ought not to be a woman," Noir warns. "You've got enough of them. And two in particular? You need to straighten that shit out. It's lucky you're only married to one. Your Thing with Hannah? I don't what you're thinking now but let that be.

"There's a line Peter Boyle used in *Hammett*. 'Back in twenty-six Sue Alabama and I nearly got married. I suppose it's just as well we didn't.'"

"Whoa," Kirkallen utters. "Strong words from our young lady but words to live by. Besides," he ventures mysteriously, "I think my idea about What's Next may appeal ... More immediately we need to find a Wi-Fi hot spot and transfer some funds into my checking account. Shire seemed happy enough to hold my check. He said something derogatory about Cedar Harbor and its lame cell access."

Marion calls from the kitchen, "Supper's ready. Anybody hungry?"

"Those ladies," Noir remarks, "they know their way around a stove."

"I think Marion has a lot to do with that," Hardy intones.

The trio and their hound file inside to join Alexandra, Elizabeth, Grace, Abby, Hannah, Heather, Olivia, Amelia, Marion, Carmody and Susannah for supper. The end of last fall's venison.

After a drawn out dinner and a communal cleanup effort they ponder the lake from the vantage of their favorite porch. Hardy pours small neat Balvenies for those who desire one.

Kirkallen demurs. "You know me," he shrugs.

The color goes out of the day at dusk. The sky assumes a gray pallor and the lake takes on a darker tint of a similar shade. A waxing crescent moon rises out of the water.

Kirkallen is thinking aloud. "I'm not looking forward to going home. I love this country."

"Interesting," Elizabeth answers. She glances meaningfully at her companions.

"Daddy," Elizabeth offers.

Her familiar use of the paternal reference startles Hardy.

"We ..." she motions to the women and leans forward to meet her father's gaze, "... we have a proposition for you and Kirkallen. Are you interested in hearing us out?"

"Do tell," Kirkallen replies.

SHE SURE MADE IT COMPLICATED

I need to test Hannah out of the gate.

We're sitting by ourselves in The Convent chapel. It's where we drove after we asked Micah and Kirkallen to live and work with us.

We're here to pray.

We like to pray together. It keeps us sane. It keeps us honest.

It's time for honesty now.

I say, "You know what we're doing is complicated? When you were young, you wanted a piece of Micah and ended up with much more than expected. You dealt with it by holding it at arm's length. You put your head down and forged ahead. Thank God your parents stood by you.

"Now your skeletons are emerging from the closet. I bet you never dreamed it would turn out like it has."

I feel her vibrating next to me. Like she's chilled.

She bows her head and places her forehead on her hands which are resting on the pew in front of us.

I ask the key question, "What are we going to do about Micah? Do you still want him?"

I give her time to soak in the shock value. I love her response.

"It's basically what I said after you challenged me when I broke the news about Grace. I want to know the person Micah is now. The person he's turned into is not the same as the guy I once thought I loved. I want to know the New Micah. So does Grace."

"So do I." There's a trace of irony in my voice.

Hannah leans her shoulder into mine. I like what she says next even better.

"I don't want any romantic piece of him. I want you to have the chance to repair your relationship. I will do everything I can to give you the space you need to fix what's injured."

She says her next piece with a stern motherly note in her voice. "If you find you can't be together as a couple you have to figure out how to be together in our larger group. We're in this Convent and House Thing together. All of us. We must get along."

"I'm not sure I can make a go of the former but I'm going to try," I say. "I think Micah will too."

"I think you're right," Hannah replies.

I continue. "About the latter? Even if we can't work Us out, I know we can do what's needed for the good of everyone. We know we have to."

"We'll have good company. God will walk with us if we let Her."

"I think God had a hand at putting this string of coincidences together. I think it's Her gift to us. She's showing us the path to healing."

"She sure made it complicated."

"We're the ones who made it complicated."

Hannah places her hand on mine and squeezes. "And we'll pray for strength and guidance to uncomplicate it."

"Amen."

I'D FRENCH KISS HER NOW

You've read this far with only slight references to cell phones and Wi-Fi reception.

That's deliberate.

Though I know mobile phones are useful, I don't like them. Neither does the Narrator. That's why the Cedar Harbor he invented doesn't have an awkward and unsightly AT&T tower looming on a nearby ridge.

I've heard the town citizenry is clamoring for one. The Installation Issue will soon appear as a New Business item on the Town Council's docket. Abby and her aldermen can deal with that.

For the time being, service is spotty. Cedar Harbor is a piece of heaven. It's removed from the reckless assault electronics has visited upon our senses. It's a beautiful thing. This is a town where people actually talk to each other.

The problem is we need immediate access. To transfer funds for Kirkallen's check to clear. It takes most of the day, a drive toward Duluth and a stop in a miniscule public library to do what needs doing. The ride in the new truck, Muskie contentedly curled between us, gives us time to talk.

We *talk* like we did when we went fishing and I scared off the eagle. In partial sentences, uncompleted thoughts and unvoiced feelings. It's easy to let Kirkallen spin it.

He says we ought to move to The House on the Hill. We owe it to ourselves. He makes a good case. The Carriage House is heated; it has two bedrooms, a living area, a kitchen and a bath.

I approach the idea indirectly. "For the first time in twenty years the house finches didn't nest on our front porch and the gold finches have deserted our feeders. I feel zero attachment to our house."

"Exactly," Kirkallen agrees, "if we move here we'll be near family too."

Kirkallen's like Muskie. She thinks she's a member of our pack. Kirkallen also thinks he belongs.

He does.

He loves Heather and her girls. He gets along with Libby and Alexandra, Hannah and Abby and Grace and Marion.

They like him.

How can they not? Kirkallen is a good man. He has a giant heart.

I tried to remember that immediately before leaving this morning when we argued about who gets to drive our new truck.

He is.

Then Kirkallen goes Navajo on me. He gives me his Family's Important Spiel. He tells me I need healing. He appends Abby and Hannah and Elizabeth to the list before reminding me I need to work at calling Libby *Elizabeth*.

His patter sounds practiced. Maybe he's told you this before?

I think he's right.

I do need healing. I need to Get Right with My Women.

I'll say that privately but sure won't admit to it if you tell them I referred to them with a possessive pronoun. At least I didn't say *girls*.

My heart pretty much shattered when I played the Total Asshole with Libby. I fell apart when Abby moved out. I zeroed out any emotional account I had.

These are things I'm barely able to say, much less to Kirkallen. Fortunately he knows me so it works. He knows it's easier for me to tell you my feelings than him. That's too darn personal.

Bottom line? What a moron I am. What morons guys can be in general.

Kirkallen says the Silverado Deal is timely. "Since we have a truck we may as well live in a place where we can use it."

This is his backhand way of saying he likes having work.

You remember he's handy with tools? He's happy to become caretaker and general troubleshooter for The Convent and the House on the Hill.

I'm actually cool with the notion of caring for the grounds at The House. There's a bonus too. I'll get to drive a tractor. I'm already thinking about converting a good piece of lawn into a wildflower sanctuary and managing the property to attract wildlife. Better not get ahead of myself ...

Our biggest concern, apart from leaving Noir, is mutual.

No it's not moving farther north into a much deeper and longer winter. Look around. It's early June and daffodils are in bloom. Get the picture? We're closer to the North Pole than the Equator.

When I remind Kirkallen about leaving our favored trout haunts—the Kinnickinnic, the Whitewater, the Rush, the Root—he takes significant pause.

"We can fish small stream brookies here," he reasons. "There are those trout-managed lakes. We can throw big flies for pike and smallies. There are steelhead runs. We can try the Big Lake for Coasters."

I take the fly he casts. "Susannah and Carmody help run that B&B over at Clear Spring. They help out at the town fly shop. They offered us room and board if we want to fish there."

Kirkallen follows my line of thinking. "We can always head to Montana."

Like I said the knottiest problem for us is Noir.

We can't quite say it to each other but we love that woman.

We couch it in awkward language. We focus on how she could look after the Saint Paul house and how we'd keep a guest cottage ready for her.

What we also can't quite admit is Noir has ridden herd on us. Kept us in line.

We're not sure what we'll do without her.

We're so blind we don't even consider she might not know what to do without us.

We settle on the notion we're not leaving Noir. Grace will move in. We'll give them the space they need to live their lives without two old geezers peering over their shoulders and folding their laundry.

That seals the deal.

We're ready to tell the ladies they've got new Carriage House tenants and property custodians.

Who knows how this is going to work. We'll never know until we try.

It's about time I took a chance. Don't you think?

Remember when Gayle Harte fired me and I said something like I didn't know whether to curse her or kiss her?

I'd French kiss her now.

THE OPPOSITE

Mom glossed over our upbringings and I think she did it deliberately. She could have said more about us as children and provided more insight into us as people. Heather and I have stayed in the background thus far. We've advanced the plot but you don't know us.

Heather was always the good girl. I was the opposite. I wasn't bad. I didn't get in trouble with the law or anything. I didn't do drugs.

I specialized in being difficult.

Willful. Headstrong.

I acted out because I could never be as good at school and sports and church and boys as my All Star Older Sister. I didn't make time for the things Heather excelled in. I didn't make time for them because I couldn't do them as well as she could. All I had time for was for my friends.

I spent a lot of time in the Penalty Box, at school and at home. That's what Dad called it.

I called myself the Queen of Study Hall Detention. And I never studied there.

And Mom and Dad were always getting after me to do something I needed to or should. Or they were making me undo something I shouldn't have done and did. We didn't have big fights or anything. We just didn't understand each other.

I think they felt relieved when I went to college.

I know I did. I was glad to go away. I needed to. I thought my parents existed to make my life difficult.

Actually the complete opposite is true. I made my parents' lives tougher than they had to be.

I see that now. I'm glad it's behind me. I'm glad I'm over it. I'm glad they love me.

Mom and I are much closer. We talk.

That's because Hannah encouraged her to talk with me to help her understand her confusion over my thing for women.

Coming Out to Mom changed our lives. She struggled with it but eventually understood. I struggled with Mom and that helped me learn to talk through issues with people I love. So My Coming Out opened both of our minds and our hearts. But that was after I turned my life around in college.

I blossomed there.

Among other things I made a better grade of friends. People who were interested in doing positive things with their lives. They're people I keep up with today. Some even attended our wedding.

Among other things I got good grades. I got good grades because I liked what I studied.

I liked better what I learned.

I liked best who I was becoming. A real person.

I'm the one who went to grad school.

That's where I went after I graduated. The graduation Dad refused to attend. The one where I surprised the heck out of Mom by walking down the commencement aisle with an Honors Medal around my neck.

My life changed even more in grad school. I met Alexandra when she came to town to visit one of my classmates. Alex invited both of us to visit her at The House on the Hill. I started going back on my own. It's there I admitted what I already knew. What Alexandra sensed.

I liked women more than men.

I told you I blossomed in college. What I know now is I blossomed after I let myself step out of Heather's shadow. It's a shadow she never deliberately cast. It's one I created so I could stand in it and be different from her.

I should tell you more about my sister. I want you to know we're good.

She was older. We were never in the same school at the same time, though we did walk the same parochial path. We were never close because of our ages and circumstances but we never had issues. We were at different times in our lives, that's all.

We're friends now. We're closer than we've ever been.

Much closer.

It's Heather who asked me if it was okay for her to invite Dad to the wedding. Or maybe it was Alexandra's idea to invite Dad that initiated it. I never thought to inquire if they told Mom or Hannah about the invitation. For that matter I never thought to ask them if Dad was coming. I assumed he was. Which is why I had a little speech prepared when he arrived.

I thought my assumption was common knowledge. I don't ever remember speaking to Mom about his coming. Hannah either. I thought they knew. From what I've heard about Hannah's Revelatory Moment? I'm guessing they didn't. But I am happy to know I have a half-sister.

Regardless of whose idea it was to invite Dad to the wedding, both Alexandra and Heather said it would be good for me. They knew I was so angry with Dad I could spit. They said I had to get over it and move on with my life. They thought the wedding was a good place to lay the groundwork.

I'd been angry at Dad for like forever. I'd let the Graduation Thing fester. I was so pissed when he didn't attend. I wanted him to come. I told Mom to invite him and she said she did.

What I understand now is I didn't want to share the joy of my graduating. I wanted to rub his nose with my Honors Medal. To prove that, like Heather, I was amounting to Something, to Someone. I got angrier when he didn't give me that chance and it sealed the deal.

The deal was mostly sealed anyway. You know I refused to go home after the embarrassing New Year's Eve Debacle.

I was stupid.

We were stupid.

And us being stupid? It killed Mom. I regret that to this very moment.

We're recovering from being stupid now.

The wedding helped.

Dad's apology totally helped.

Then he stayed for the Showdown at The Convent. I'm not sure why but he did.

So I'm ready to let bygones be bygones.

But it was Alexandra's and Heather's and Noir's doing that got me thinking about inviting Dad and Kirkallen to live and work with us.

Alexandra regrets she wasn't closer to her parents. She was in France when they ran off the road, not quite avoiding the deer they tried to miss. She pines for them more than she admits. Since Alexandra doesn't have the opportunity to be around her parents, she says I should make the most of my opportunity. She says she thinks Dad and I have stayed apart for so long out of sheer stubbornness. She says that's a stupid reason. She called me a *blockhead*.

It's true.

Heather says asking Dad and Kirkallen to join us is an effective means of putting Mom and Dad in the same place at the same time. She thinks if they can work as part of a group for the good of The House on the Hill and The Convent that they can have something else to focus on and that will let time heal the wounds they inflicted on each other.

She says everybody does that to people they love. She says they'll get over it.

Noir approached it from a different angle. Though she likes to tease Kirkallen unmercifully, it's how she tells him she loves him. But she listens to the man. She's been talking to me about walking in beauty and making my life whole.

I get a kick out of her using wisdom she's heard from Kirkallen. But I know she's right.

Noir also said something really interesting. Something I hadn't thought about before and now believe to be true.

I think the anger Dad felt toward me about the New Year's Eve Thing and My Subsequent Departure was misplaced.

What was really going on is he was angry with himself. Angry because he'd disappointed himself. Disappointed because he let himself do a job he despised. One he despised for far too long. Disappointed because he was letting his daughters down by being less of a man than he could. Disappointed because he was setting a poor example for his girls.

He was angry he'd turned into an Ordinary Man. He thinks his life has not mattered.

Since he couldn't express his anger and keep working, he expressed it by keeping his distance from me. Heather was already out of the house.

So the main reason we asked Dad to come live and work with us at The House is to help him get over being angry with himself.

Kirkallen's providing assistance but that's something he understands on a very superficial level. He is, after all, a guy. They have their limitations. But in spite of his shortcomings, Kirkallen is a good man, I admit that. I'm saying I don't think he realizes how much we manipulate him.

I'm glad Noir's Lads have accepted our offer. In fact I'm delighted.

I'll give them time to settle in but I've got plans for Dad. I'll eventually rope him into working with Alexandra and me. We're taking over Mom's and Hannah's syrup chores. We're inaugurating a modest organic produce business. You know, kales and lettuces and herbs and mustards and collards and root vegetables and squashes. Things like that. Locally sourced farm-to-table products are the rage now.

We can cash in.

Alexandra and I have been talking and scheming on that score. We've been talking with Heather and Mom and Hannah and Grace and Noir too. We'll tell you more about that later.

EIGHT

THE BEAUTY WAY

I STILL DON'T KNOW WHAT I BELIEVE

I still don't know what I believe. I suppose I never will.

In telling this story, I planned to delve into more detail about my skepticism and believing. Kind of like John Irving did in *A Prayer for Owen Meany*. But I'm not nearly a good enough writer or thinker for that.

I hoped to include items like wishing Jesus had stuck around after the Resurrection to see the job through. He could've helped us play things out for the best. You'd think he would have taken a hint from the Old Testament. Consider all the covenants the people of God broke in that book. Jesus should have known better.

If Jesus had remained on earth we'd also know much more clearly what he said and did. Those four gospel writers gave it a good shot but they put marbles in their Lord's mouth. Especially with that *In the beginning was Word* stuff. John must've had a good stash.

As it stands we've been fighting forever over Who We Believe In, How We Believe and Who Believes the Right Way. We've killed a multitude of folks in the name of God.

What a waste.

A shame.

I hope God's ashamed for letting it happen. He should be.

As to the many who like to talk and think and write about God?

There are those who think Deep Thoughts. So-called philosophers and theologians and academics, people whom I consider with moderate bemusement as they occupy their lives and minds with a kind of mental masturbation. Though I suspect they're leery of people like me who disregard their very basic assumptions, I'm content to let them think and write and speak those Deep Thoughts. Somebody should. I only hope they understand the enormous privilege institutions like universities and churches give them to do so.

By now it is apparent I do not think deep thoughts.

I cannot think deep thoughts.

Though I love to read, I confess I cannot read some of the great writers. Like those well-known twentieth century guys. Joyce, Faulkner, Proust, Pound, Kafka and Mann.

I prefer to keep it simple. I prefer to eat the icing off the cake. So I'll think no deeper. It's not getting me anywhere. I'll let sleeping dogs lie.

I can tell you I still can't pray. Not with any honesty in my heart. Maybe I don't know how. You already know I don't want to trouble an all-powerful deity with my petty cares and concerns. He's got much bigger issues to deal with. Read the newspaper headlines. They're enough to frighten anyone.

If you allow for prayers of thanks, I do say those. I am indeed grateful for the many blessings in my life. For the good and bad fortune that has come to me. I'm not quite sure Whom I'm thanking but it feels good anyway.

My temple is larger now. I'd never think to criticize others' belief in God and Christ. I completely understand how my circle of women friends at the House on the Hill and over at The Convent—an ex-lover, a spouse, daughters of all sorts, friends, acquaintances—can place their trust in a Living God. I admire them for doing so. Like Kirkallen said, they are stronger, braver, smarter and wiser than I. They are more completely Whole than I can ever be.

So I am content to stop asking God Questions. Asking has gotten me in trouble. I think I understand I'll never get a satisfactory answer anyway.

I'll leave it with the notion that we all live and love imperfectly. Didn't Grace say something like that?

It's a good line.

I'm the poster boy for it.

So is God. As much as we need His help, He needs ours. If He lives, He lives and loves imperfectly too.

And, before my lady friends object, I will say I can't for the life of me understand why well-meaning Christian women would want to claim that God is female. I'll say again God has to be a He because a Female Almighty would have done a much better job making this world work how it ought to.

In the end I know I don't Believe Right. Or nearly enough. But I know I believe sufficiently to serve those who do.

I also know all humans need to recognize a Creator. Perhaps to justify their existence. Perhaps not. Who knows for sure?

I know I don't.

What I do know is that humans believe in different ways. I'm content to believe that we discover truths in many ways and through assorted sages.

As far as that goes, all I can utter is a prayer of thanks.

THANK YOU, KRISTA

I no longer listen to National Public Radio. Not since The Election. As much as I agreed with what reporters said about the Republican Candidate, they put a huge target on his back. I thought they treated him unfairly. Even though the guy deserved it.

But it is embarrassing to have to call a real estate broker *president*.

I've also come to believe most of our political leaders are selfish and self-serving. They'll willingly promise you what you want to hear.

Once elected? They'll go rogue on you.

They'll raise your taxes, then profligately spend the proceeds. They'll lie and cheat to get what they want—except they can't get it now because the principal political parties are too intent on fighting each other to accomplish anything. It's a ridiculous state of affairs.

Because the reports about the world and national news are so depressing, I've resorted to listening to sports talk radio and to the pundits who are so sincerely and passionately outfitted with pompous opinions and obscure facts about truly insignificant and entirely absurd topics.

I understand America's Obsession with Sport is—or should be—alarming.

I'm blown away by how many Americans care so fervidly about college football. People who'd pay a couple hundred bucks for a seat in a stadium on a Saturday afternoon and wouldn't walk across the street to buy a homeless person a meal.

I have, however, come to respect the sports talk show hosts for taking their work so seriously and professionally. They know their stuff. Whereas the World of NPR News is so ridiculous it's sad, the World of Sport is so ridiculous it's laughable.

I'd rather laugh than cry.

When I did listen to public radio there was a time I enjoyed *On Being*, Krista Tippett's program devoted to All Things Spiritual. She gradually wore me down. She overwhelmed me with her sincerity. It felt overplayed and I began to suspect her motives. I suspect she chuckles on the frequent trips she takes to make bank deposits. At least I hope she does. She's created a good gig for herself. And people like her.

But the other morning the alarm radio popped on in time for me to hear her opening a show with a quote from Thomas Merton, a deceased Trappist monk, an ordained Catholic priest, a social activist and theologian who died when I was courting Hannah Penner.

The gift of his words—and thank you, Krista, for sharing—provides me with food for thought. And action.

"It is true that we are called to create a better world but we are first of all called to a more immediate and exalted task, that of creating our own lives."

Words to live by.

I never found What I Wanted, What I Wanted to Do and Who I Wanted to Do It With.

It's time to start.

I have that opportunity in the freedom granted by Gayle Harte and in the grace granted to me by the women at The House on the Hill. Doc Stone said it best. I have about eighteen years left. Eighteen years to live a more complete and fulfilling life.

Now you know more about my life than I've ever told anyone and I don't even know you. For that matter I now know more about me than I've ever told myself.

Say hello to the New Me.

Kirkallen and I are happy at The House on the Hill. It's given us purpose. So much so, we don't need the Balvenie or the pot. Well … we take an occasional hit. We love a good buzz. And they don't call it the Water of Life without good reason. But most of all we're happy to feel wanted, needed and useful. We're happy to like and be liked.

Dare I say love and be loved?

We're gettin' our *hozro* on. And I'm busy creating the New Me, which depends so vitally on the love and care others show for me. I'm ready to show it back.

I'VE RUN OUT OF HILLERMAN BOOKS

We've settled in since The Wedding and Subsequent Convent Revival. Hardy and I are familiar faces in town and at The Convent. Storekeepers like us because we bring them business and because we're friendly guys. There are times when I think I'm the first African-American man some of them have known. That's not bad either.

I've opened several local accounts, including Amundsen's Hardware, Fuel, Hunting & Fishing Emporium where I have two—one for goods and necessaries and one for fuel. Cedar County Bank keeps my money.

We've purchased a co-op membership. We buy fresh herring off the dock. Milwaukee and Violet welcome us at their brewery. We're regulars at Big Lake Coffee & Beans and the Blue Plate Diner. The Sisters seem to like us too. But hey, we're likeable guys and we like to be liked by ladies.

At our ages it's what we have left. That and our pipe dreams.

What we also have that we don't tell them is we know they think they've got us thinking we're helping them when actually they think they're helping us.

Hardy and I know—and don't share—one Big Secret.

We're each helping the other.

That's a good way to be.

I like how it's working out even though I've run out of Hillerman books. I've read them all. The stories are interesting and the Navajo tidbits he doles out have helped me grow.

Tony's gone. He died in 2008. Rest in peace. Even though I never knew him I would have liked to sit and visit. Maybe we'll meet in a different world.

I'm reading like a champ now. That's what I do with my evenings. Especially without cable and reliable Web access. Hardy ties the flies. I do the reading. And I read aloud to my friends.

I've given up on Pema Chodrön. She's one Deep Lady. Too deep for me. It takes too darn much work to do all that meditating and introspecting stuff. All I need is to occasionally light one up.

I've entered a New Phase. I'm traveling the globe with Paul Theroux. He's an educated and likeable fellow. He's opening all sorts of worlds and cultures to me. He's got me interested in a new line of thinking. I won't abandon the Navajo Way entirely. Particularly since I need to learn to let people finish speaking before I respond. But I'm liking something I found in *The Ghost Train to the Eastern Star*. I'm studying a creed much older than Christianity, dating as far back as three thousand years.

Zoroastrianism.

It's monotheistic. The chief prophet, Zarathustra, treated men and women equally. He had absolutely no use for priests as intercessors. He abhorred animal sacrifice, steered clear of evangelism and didn't believe in miracles other than the miracle of creation.

He loved light and fire. How can you not dig that?

Plus he lived by three basic principles.

Good thoughts.

Good words.

Good deeds.

He's not too far removed from my bud's namesake, the Old Testament prophet Micah. His popular verse is about the only one worth remembering in the whole Christian Bible. Something like doing justice, loving kindness, walking humbly with your god.

Between these guys—a wise man who lived three millennia ago and a guy who prophesied in the Southern Kingdom maybe about 720 BCE—I have what I need. Especially since I have all my women to care for.

While I look after the Sisters and Marion and keep Alexandra and Elizabeth and Abby and Hannah honest at The House on the Hill, I'll let them think they're looking after me—and that allows me to focus on Hardy.

He's healing, starting a new life. He loves driving the tractor and working the grounds. He's tying for a small fly shop in Cedar Harbor that opened about a month ago. He's becoming a much better fisherman. Funny how that goes. The less you care about catching fish? The more you catch 'em.

I know Hardy saved my life when he pulled me out from under the Burnside Bridge. And Hardy more clearly understands what Noir already knows. He's lucky to have found us.

Speaking of Noir? That's the problem with living here.

I miss the hell out of that girl.

I love her.

Maybe I should tell her that.

What do you think?

If I am truly walking the Beauty Way I must.

❖

WE HAVE THE LADS WHERE WE WANT THEM

You read the chapter title.

We do have The Lads where we want them.

You've just heard from my former housemates, Hardy and Kirkallen. You listened to them get misty about their new lives at The Convent and The House on the Hill. You listened to them tell how they like being Caretakers for their women.

They think they had something to do with making it happen.

What happened is a bunch of ladies much smarter than them made it happen. It started when Heather and I connived to get Hardy to the wedding.

Heather and I knew about Elizabeth's sexual preference. We never worried it would put Hardy off his game but we didn't share the fact because we didn't want to muddy the waters. It was easy to obscure the facts. Especially since The Lads are easy to misdirect. All you need to do is send them fishing.

Though Elizabeth and Alexandra did give us the Go Ahead with inviting Hardy to their wedding, they didn't know Heather and I had more detailed plans. For starters we didn't tell them if Hardy agreed to attend and they never asked. They were too absorbed in the planning details. We dropped just enough hints to make sure Elizabeth wouldn't lose it if Hardy showed.

I'm thinking she'd thought about what to say. She was fantastic.

Then there was that Out of the Blue Curveball. The Hannah and Grace and Abby and Hardy Connection. That appears to be working out too.

It all seems to be working out.

The bottom line is The Lads are happy to work for us. I'll get to how I'm included in *Us* in a minute. Let's just let them think Guy Thoughts about being useful to and needed by Their Women.

We are guiding them. And they don't even know it.

This is Noir again. You should know it turns out Grace and I are good friends. She's sorta the mother figure I miss. I'm the sister-daughter she never had.

She and Heather and I are making more plans. This time we included Hannah and Abby and Elizabeth and Alexandra and a couple of others too.

The Lads don't know I've submitted my resignation to St. Rose. They don't know I'll be working for Milwaukee and Violet at the brewery. They need a technology geek and want me.

The Lads don't know I'm going to help Elizabeth and Alexandra with their organic garden project. Maybe with the syruping too. I'd like to put an entry into the State Fair competition one day.

The boys also don't know they don't have to spruce up one of the guest cabins at The House for me like they do when I visit. Alexandra and Elizabeth and Hannah and Abby have invited me to live with them in the Big House. Marion's set up a room.

What about Grace? The Lads don't know Heather's put Hardy and Abby's Saint Paul home on the market. Once it sells Grace will move up too. We'll convince Hardy to hand over the house sale proceeds to create a nonprofit she'll run with her mother and stepmother. Since Abby's agreed to the sale terms Hardy will fall in line.

And don't worry about The Lads' financial future. We've got that covered. Abby and Hannah made a literal fortune. Alexandra's not poor; she knows money management. Elizabeth's done alright on her own.

In *Dial M for Murder* Robert Cummings's character describes how "in stories things usually turn out the way the author wants them to; and in real life they don't ... always."

In the instance of this story the ending is happy.

I think that's how the Narrator meant it to turn out. Trouble is he lost control a long time ago.

This has turned into Our Story and the ending isn't happening by chance. A bunch of tough smart women are making it happen. I'm delighted they invited me to join them.

Now I have a home. And a Family. And if you didn't already Get It, there's more than blood to a family connection.

The Family at the House on the Hill is living proof of that.

As to my friend Hardy? He's finding his way, which is good. Though he's stopped *asking* his God Questions I know he's *thinking* them.

The funny thing? As deep as His Doubt runs he's fond of the old Christian hymns he grew up with. *Be Thou My Vision, Praise My Soul the King of Heaven, Crown Him with Many Crowns,* that sort of thing. He's ripped them to Media Player and Kirkallen tells me Hardy often plays them on Sunday mornings as he sips light coffee and reads his fishing books.

The ultimate irony is his very favorite is *The Church's One Foundation.* It's a lovely poetic song, written in the 1860s by Samuel Stone. If you know the hymn, you know how the title line ends.

"… is Jesus Christ her Lord."

So the man who so deeply questions Jesus? His favorite hymn acknowledges Him as Lord.

Regardless of what you make of Hardy's Spiritual Questioning, he's finally figured out life works better if you stop asking Heavy Questions and simply get on with the Living Each Day to Its Potential.

That's the truth of it.

We have The Lads where we want them.

We want them with us. And they want to be there.

We strong women will keep them on the right path.

HELPING THE HELPER

I am my father's daughter. I see it now.

Let me explain.

What can I tell you about my life except I was born with a silver spoon in my mouth and didn't blow it? In fact I took advantage. Libby is right. I was the All Star Older Sister.

I only regret Libby felt as overshadowed as she did. I'm glad she doesn't now.

Unlike Libby I needed to be liked.

I did what I was told and I did it when I was told to do it. I did my homework, got good grades and played sports well. I spent years as an altar server. I played the piano and gave recitals. I never got in trouble. I stayed away from drugs. Mom and Dad never objected to my boyfriends.

I went to college for free and I made Daddy particularly proud by making the basketball team. I liked that he was proud but I liked playing better. And I graduated in four years.

I didn't go to grad school. I kind of *had* to get married. Fortunately I loved Kyle and he loved me. We did a courthouse ceremony in San Diego and moved to Saint Paul where I had Olivia. I made motherhood fit with selling homes and eventually started my own agency.

Even though I didn't marry a Catholic in a Catholic church that turned out okay too. Kyle took the RCIA and goes to Mass with us. Olivia and Amelia are confirmed. They've sensibly kept boys at distance. They're good students and are talking about college.

I've got a good life. I have everything I want and need.

That's why I'm going to turn it upside down.

I've worked behind the scenes in this story. I've said some things, kept the action moving, but I did it quietly while I schemed and planned and whispered behind closed doors. I've helped put everyone in a better position than when we started. I think people are healing.

It's all worked pretty much as I hoped. If they're not already, all the moving pieces will soon be living Up North. And that result is something I planned with an ulterior motive. Something I've kept in the back of my mind. It's something I've never confided. Not even to Mom or Libby or Noir or Grace.

I'm going to join them.

We're going to join them.

You know Noir and Grace and Libby and Alexandra and Hannah and Abby are conspiring with our plan to sell my folks' Saint Paul home. You know we've agreed about doling out the proceeds.

They don't know I'm putting our home on the market.

Like Daddy, I'd rather live in the country.

This is the simplest piece of my tripart reasoning. I have two other concerns.

I don't want to be the Outrider in our larger family group. I don't want to be the only City Dweller. I want to be part of their lives. I want my girls to relate to their relatives, blood or otherwise, in a deeper richer way.

Kyle's down with it. He'll move when we're ready. He says he can paint anywhere. He believes Cedar Harbor's a great place to base a photography business. He says the lake and sky are full of light. He says Monet would've loved Lake Superior's moods.

Olivia and Amelia admit they'll miss their friends but they love thinking about being in on the action at The Convent and The House on the Hill. I've heard them use Noir's phrase. They like the Estrogenic Energy. Though I'm surprised by how easily they agreed to the move I think it shows how tight we are as a group. Remind me to say a prayer of thanks for that.

It will take time. We'll let the girls complete the coming academic year in Saint Paul. I'll put our house on the market in the spring. It should move quickly as will my parents' place.

I'll start closing out my business. I can find work Up North. Lake Country Realty is making overtures. I know that because we've begun looking for a house and have talked with them. I don't know if we'll buy or build. We'll figure that out. I hope to move next summer.

One of the best ironies about moving? I'll be moving to a place where Libby already casts a shadow. You can call it payback but I'm the one who needs payment.

Why?

I sound too good to be true, don't I? My life sounds too good to be true.

I need healing. I carry some hurt I haven't mentioned, something I came to understand when I said *I am my father's daughter.*

Something I didn't see until Daddy made his Recent Break.

Like him, I did what I believed I was expected to do. I dotted each *I,* crossed every *T.*

Sure I did a more efficient job than Daddy. He can still beat me at H-O-R-S-E. He still has a sweet outside touch and I was a post player.

But I stayed married. Kyle and I are solid. I love him. He acts like he loves me.

Daddy's right. He says I'm lucky my girls love me and talk to me and I know it. There's no rift like the one he and Libby are mending.

Unlike Daddy I mostly like my job. When people do business with me they generally walk away happy—and with a new place to call *home*. It's rewarding on an emotional level. It's also rewarding financially. I make more than I ought. We're not rolling in dough but we have more than enough. I can afford to send my girls to college. I own a Mercedes and I love driving it.

Like Daddy though, I am a spiritual electron. There's a void in my heart.

I live vicariously. I live through others. I said it before: I need to be liked.

I need to learn to live for myself too. I need to put my needs forward. Pursue my own agenda. Given time I think I can work that out.

The only way I know to start healing is to become an integral part of our larger family group. Especially one that functions organically and peaceably. I feel best when I'm part of it. I look forward to taking my beauty walk.

When I played ball in San Diego my coach placed special emphasis on his defensive scheme. We worked on Team Defense every day in practice. It's a system where each player is asked to help out, to cover for her teammate when the person her teammate's guarding gets past her.

When the first player helps, the whole team must react because the Helper has left the player she's guarding. The next player has to help her.

Coach called it *Helping the Helper.*

Helping the Helper.

I like that.

You see how I'm looking at it? I've helped my friends and family start down a good path. Now it's time for me to head down that path too.

It's time for them to start helping me.

I think they will.

❖

BLESS THEM ALL

What remains when all is said and mostly done?

Micah Hardy's settled in to North Country Living. He's content with his circumstances.

It's late evening and he sits alone on The House veranda. He's savoring the quiet, the lake and the sky. He idly considers a collection of facts and feelings and thoughts and realities.

Elizabeth is happy with her new life. As is Alexandra. He wishes them all the happiness in the world. They are scheming to fund an organic garden business and they've asked him to grow wildflowers for them. They're taking over Abby and Hannah's maple syrup gig. They've got each other. That counts for a lot.

More than they can measure.

Hardy's delighted Libby has allowed him to return to her good graces. Graciously too. Hardy's grateful she has a forgiving heart. He vows silently from this moment forward to always act to keep her trust.

Keep reminding him however. He needs to remember to call her *Elizabeth*. If nothing else it's a matter of respect. Hardy's struggle has deep roots. Sometimes he sees the little girl he called by another name. The pigtail version he taught to turn cartwheels.

Abby and Hannah have their convent back. They are continuing their good work and deeds. Hardy is pleased they've created meaningful lives for themselves—and that they're instrumental in helping others create meaningful lives. They no longer have skeletons they keep in their closets. They are competent principled women. They are Women of Faith. If they believe in asking their God for strength and guidance, Hardy's good with that.

What about Hardy and Abby?

They have work to do.

I have to leave that up to them. One thing though? Hardy must avoid overanalyzing his God Confusions with Abby. He has to remember what he said earlier about swearing off those questions.

As it stands each is comforted by knowing, at minimum, they can be friends. Especially since Hardy thinks he still loves Abby and Abby thinks she still loves Hardy.

Does love come without friendship? Does love have to come out of friendship? It is going to be interesting for them to answer those questions. They'll start doing that in the next book.

Hannah? The best part is she's no longer fixed in Hardy's mind as a comely coed. He sees her fully now. He likes the Person She Has Become much better than the One He Knew. She is tough and smart and strong. She's also smart enough to look to the group, and to her God, for healing. She carried her Private Grief far too long.

Hardy and Hannah are working at forming a healthy friendship, one each secretly hopes grows much deeper and more meaningful than the one they built in their youth. They're much better equipped to do that now. I hope they flourish.

Let's be honest though. Hardy will always harbor a slight resentment toward her for holding out on telling him about Grace.

He would have liked to know.

He needs to listen to Kirkallen.

For all the grief Hardy gives him, he does heed his good friend. Hardy understands there's a bit of Seer in the man. So he's attentive when he's reminded how the Navajo Walk in Beauty by learning to let go of old resentments.

He has a reason to let go. He and Hannah have a reason to work at being friends.

They have a daughter they love.

Grace? Hardy's over the moon with finding her.

As far as he's concerned he hopes she visits often. He hopes the Mennonites let her keep ministering in spite of their doctrinal differences. Hardy hopes they understand how stupid they'd be to lose her. Though Hardy knows Abiding Strictly by Church Polity has not stopped churches from acting irrationally in the past, he is content to let them figure it out. He's confident Grace will land on her feet.

What he doesn't know is the conference committee's decision doesn't matter. He doesn't know about Grace's plan to join The Family at The House. He doesn't know his wish to see his new daughter more frequently will soon be granted.

What about Kirkallen?

Hardy's delighted his friend has found renewed purpose in his caretaker work. He's positively blossoming in the North Country. He's biking his butt off. He's climbed Eagle Mountain, Minnesota's highest peak. Like Hardy he's delighted to be among the company of women. He is walking in beauty.

Hardy frets for Noir. He doesn't know how long she can last at her admissions job. Wherever she ends up he'll always treat her as a daughter. He passionately hopes wherever she ends up is not far removed.

The last time she visited he mentioned she needed to find a friend to walk through life with. He deliberately chose the word *friend*, keeping the gender neutral.

She said she was working on it.

Hardy knows enough to know she'll say more when she's ready.

Not before.

Hardy understands she effectively and protectively hides her own self. She needs healing too.

He knows as long as she stays near Her Extended Family they'll allow her the space she needs. But let's face it, Hardy misses the heck out of her. Muskie too.

Hardy will be more than pleased when Noir tells him she's joining the clan.

Heather remains Hardy's constant. Of all the women in his life she sees him the most clearly for who he is. She allows him the space to breathe as she continues to talk and fish with him.

He does harbor a small piece of worry about her.

He thinks they're too much alike.

She works too hard at being liked.

Hardy thinks she needs to look out for herself. He makes a mental note to talk to her about that. He hopes she'll listen.

He doesn't know Heather's begun putting Her Plan into action. He'll be psyched.

First thing he'll do is take her fishing.

Let's close this on a lighter note.

What about the ghost, or ghosts, of the Family Kerr?

When she visits, Muskie doesn't lie on the porch glider as much as she used to. When she does, she uses the entire area. In fact it's the only piece of furniture, other than Noir's bed, she does use. It no longer glides on its own. Since The House on the Hill has found new life and The Convent is in secure hands, the Kerr spirits are at peace.

As best as this oddly interconnected family can humanly manage, they are all finding distinct measures of peace.

Bless them all. Thank them all.

"TRYIN' TO BE AN UPRIGHT MAN"

You're not done yet.

No that's not right. What I mean is *I'm not done yet*. Not quite.

I can't let the Narrator have the last words. He left you by describing how I'm perceiving my important relationships, my externalities.

He failed to tell you anything real about me.

I think he told it that way on purpose. To see if I'd take the challenge. I think he wanted to see if the New Me would tell you about me.

Here goes.

I want to start the ending by referring you to the opening in section three. The one where the Narrator details the many ways I am a good man. Things like paying my bills on time, never carrying a credit card balance, delivering Meals on Wheels, composting, recycling, retrieving river trash, holding the door for you, remembering your name, obeying the speed limit, liking fishing and birding, mostly being circumspect.

I am those things.

I do those things.

There is however one dramatic change.

I'm starting to live a genuine life.

I've enlarged my temple.

I've embraced Thomas Merton's "more immediate and exalted task." I'm beginning to create my own life.

I am no longer living the lie described in part three. I have purpose. In fact I have more than enough purposes to live for. What I now clearly understand is that as awkward and uncertain as I feel around my Good Women of Faith, it goes to show you that a person with the faith life of a flea can find a way to serve.

Since I've come to this realization and no longer fret over My Faith and Belief Struggles, I'm more than comfortable with accepting the notion I'll never get any definitive answers. I know I can't find them. I am content with doing as Kirkallen counseled on the afternoon we first arrived at The House when I expressed my anxiety about reuniting with Elizabeth.

"Don't force it, my brother. Let it come to you. In due time ..."

I am doing just that. The Truths I seek will arrive in due time.

Or they won't.

I know Noir's told you about how I enjoy the old hymns, the traditional Protestant standards.

Abide with Me.

Holy, Holy, Holy, Lord God Almighty.

Oh, Worship the King.

All Creatures of our God and King.

She is correct. I do like those older melodies. I savor the dated poetic language.

But lately I've been listening to more modern spiritual tunes. I'm especially taken by an upbeat one from a CD titled *Lifted, Songs of the Spirit*. There's a line in one song I love.

"Lord, I'm doin' the best I can, tryin' to be an upright man."

That's the real truth of it.

NINE

AUTHOR'S NOTE

"I'VE GOT TO DO THINGS A CERTAIN WAY"

I'd planned to write an introduction to this tale until I remembered I seldom read introductions, prefaces or prologues when I begin a new book. I prefer to encounter the volume without explanation or caveat. I'd rather let the writer do the talking. I typically get to the prefaces when I've finished. Consequently, I'm including these Afterthoughts.

If you've read this far, you should know this narrative is the product of Avoidance. I started the project about a decade ago and almost immediately ran into difficulties. I didn't like what I was writing. Although I based this novel on a different premise than my first two, I discovered I was writing it the same way I'd written the previous books. The process and product bored me. So I set it aside and only occasionally revisited it.

Then I retired and I wanted to try to be a better writer. I knew I needed to practice. I knew I wanted to find a less didactic and more conversational voice. So before I started working on something that really mattered to me (which I will), something I really want to write well, I decided to restart this story. If I could find a different way to tell it, I'd finish it.

Just for practice.

So that's what this is—a practice piece, and an expensive one at that. It took about two years of concentrated writing bursts, allowing for fermentation between the bursts. I'm glad I persevered.

This was fun to write.

I'm not exactly sure where my stories come from but I've found the best way for me to get started is to take an autobiographical premise from one of my many professional missteps. That's where this one began. I gave Micah Hardy an unsatisfactory position like one I held— about which I heard countless people say, "I could never do your job." That's all you need to know.

The rest? I knew I wanted to write about a place I called The House on the Hill. I knew I wanted a Superior setting. I also knew I wanted to include movie quotes and a dog who could see ghosts. That's not much to go on but it's what I had. So I invented a story and asked the characters to do the talking for me.

I didn't outline a plot. I wasn't sure where or how it would end. I relied on the characters to tell me where to take them. The only character that's not imagined is the dog. Muskie was a runt-of-the-litter brindle hound I loved in my youth. She stuck to me like Velcro. I don't think she saw ghosts though.

Essentially then, the book you hold in your hand is the product of my stubbornness. And as you have assuredly seen, you know I am not a good writer. I know this because my first semester English professor told me I'd never be one. I also know this because I've read what I've written in the second decade of the twenty-first century. But I wasn't about to let that deter me. I carry no illusions about being a legitimate writer, a person who produces literature. There's little, if anything, in this work you'd consider literate. I just like to write. I like a good story.

I am an author.

Anyone willing to put words on a page can do that.

And I am.

I could have asked for editorial help and suggestions but I have less than zero interest in joining a writing group. Writing for me is a solitary vacation.

I also didn't want to watch a copyreader take a red pen to the text and offer, with all sincere intent, an assortment of sage and legitimate suggestions. I knew I'd very likely reject them and blithely ignore them. So why bother?

Because this is exclusively My Project, I have written this the way I want. There's a certain freedom in it which I really like. Thus my sparse use of punctuation is a deliberate choice, as is the liberal employment of capitalization. That freedom is also based on the reality that any sane agent or editor would reject this manuscript out of hand. I'm too old and out of touch to garner any following. I paid to publish this book because I derive a certain satisfaction from completing a project and seeing the final result. So what if the effort I make to market it is minimal? That's not the point. And if you think it is, then you don't understand why I write.

I hope you liked this story. If you did, feel free to tell me. If you didn't, I'd rather you not say anything—but really, I can live with your opinion one way or the other. I'm the person I wrote this book for.

If you asked Noir about my writing style she'd probably have a quote ready. Maybe from *Where the Sidewalk Ends*, a 1950 Otto Preminger film starring Dana Andrews and Gene Tierney.

"Don't ask any questions. I've got to do things a certain way."

END

ABOUT THE AUTHOR

John Hershey's professional life unfolded in the form of five collegiate administrative, teaching and coaching stops. He has lived in Saint Paul for more than thirty years where he's grateful to share a home with his wife who continues to love him. He is the author of two novels, *Window Dressing* and *The Healing Stone*, and a family history and remembrance, *Geographic Genealogy*. His work has appeared in fly-fishing, athletic and university publications.

Printed in the United States
By Bookmasters